"I acted on impulse. I'm sorry. Is there anything I can do to make it up to you?" Rosie asked.

"Well, we're going to have to come up with a plausible story or the whole thing falls apart, and I'm not about to let that happen," Matteo said.

"Because of this deal you're working on?"

"I just need to get past the finishing line." His dark eyes were lazy and thoughtful. "So I'll be meeting the family," he murmured.

"You don't have to. I could tell them that you've been called away on business. If you disappear, then there won't be the complication of your meeting my parents. That way...I can gradually warn them that the big romance isn't actually going as planned," she thought aloud.

"And that's exactly what will happen," Matteo said soothingly. "But for the moment, that solution is off the cards."

"Why?"

"Because my deal hasn't been finalized. Until signatures are on the dotted line, we're in love. Once everything's signed, then the hasty unraveling of our relationship can begin." He gave an elegant shrug that implied that was the way forward and there was nothing she could do about it.

Cathy Williams can remember reading Harlequin books as a teenager, and now that she is writing them, she remains an avid fan. For her, there is nothing like creating romantic stories and engaging plots, and each and every book is a new adventure. Cathy lives in London, and her three daughters—Charlotte, Olivia and Emma—have always been, and continue to be, the greatest inspirations in her life.

Visit the Author Profile page
at Harlequin.com for more titles.

Cathy Williams

—

THE ITALIAN'S CHRISTMAS PROPOSITION

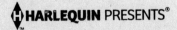

HARLEQUIN PRESENTS®

Recycling programs
for this product may
not exist in your area.

ISBN-13: 978-1-335-53882-6

The Italian's Christmas Proposition

First North American publication 2019

Copyright © 2019 by Cathy Williams

This edition published by arrangement with Harlequin Books S.A.

For questions and comments about the quality of this book, please contact us at CustomerService@Harlequin.com.

Printed in U.S.A.

www.Harlequin.com

THE ITALIAN'S
CHRISTMAS
PROPOSITION

CHAPTER ONE

'ROSIE! ARE YOU going to focus on what I'm telling you?'

The cut-glass accent was a mix of despair, impatience and long-suffering love and Rosie guiltily dragged her eyes away from the far more stimulating sight below of people coming and going, skis on shoulders, imbued with the unique excitement of being on holiday in the run-up to Christmas.

The luxury five-star resort—a jewel nestled in the heart of the Dolomitic Alps in the Veneto region of northern Italy—was the last word in the very best that money could buy and as good as a second home to Rosie, who had been coming here with her family for as long as she could remember. She could close her eyes and accurately visualise every beam of deep burnished wood, every swirl and curve of marble, the timeless cool greys of the exquisite indoor swimming pool area and the oversized chandeliers dominating the Michelin-starred restaurants.

Right now, sitting in the galleried landing with a *latte* in front of her, Rosie was in prime position to admire the dramatic twenty-foot Christmas tree sweeping upwards by the reception desk, a vision of tasteful pink and ivory and tiny little electric candles. She could almost *smell* the pine needles.

'Of course I am,' she said with a suitable level of sincerity and enthusiasm. Across from her, her sister was on the verge of another of her laborious, long-suffering sighs. 'You were asking me what I intend to do once the ski season is over. I don't *know,* Diss. Right now, I'm just enjoying the ski instructing. It's *fun.* I'm meeting some really lovely people and plus, let's not forget, I'm looking after Mum and Dad's chalet while I'm here. Making sure it…er…doesn't get burgled… or anything…'

'Because burglars are a dime a dozen here in Cortina?'

'Who knows?'

'You can't keep flitting from place to place and from job to job for ever, Rosie. You're going to be twenty-four on your next birthday and Mum and Dad…well, *all* of us— me, Emily, Mum, Dad…we're *all* concerned that it's getting to a point where you can't even be bothered to try and…you know what I mean…'

'Become an accountant? Get a mortgage? Find a decent man to look after me?' Rosie flushed and looked away. She was particularly sensitive on the subject of men and, in her heart, she knew that this was what her parents were worried about—that she was never going to find Mr Right, as both her sisters had. That she was going to spend her life drifting from Mr Wrong to Mr Really Bad Idea to Mr Will Take Advantage. She had, as it happened, been down several of those roads in the past and, whilst she had put a cheerful face on each and every disappointment, each and every one had hurt.

At this point in time, if she never had another relationship in her life again, she wouldn't lose sleep over it. The last guy she had gone out with had been a fellow traveller in India. He had been out there buying cheap Asian artefacts to sell for a profit in a market somewhere near Aldershot. They had had fun before he had taken a shine to a tall brunette and disappeared with her, leaving only an apologetic note in his wake.

The only saving grace in all these disappointing relationships, as far as Rosie was concerned, was that she hadn't made the mistake of bed-hopping. One guy. That was it. The one guy all those years ago who had broken her heart. She'd been nineteen and finding her feet all over again, having dropped out of university, and he had been there to catch her as she was falling. A biker with a refreshing disdain for convention and the first guy who had been a world away from the upper-class posh boys she had spent a lifetime meeting. She had loved everything about him, from his tattoos to the ring in his ear.

He, in the end, had loved the financial package she came with more than he had loved her for who she was, and had thrown a fit when she had promised to dump all her worldly goods for him. She still shuddered when she thought about what could have been the biggest mistake of her life. Since then, she'd enjoyed life without getting in too deep.

'Whoever said anything about becoming an accountant?' Candice rolled her eyes and grinned, and Rosie grinned back, because Emily's husband, wonderful as he was, could be a little tedious when he began pontificating about exchange rates and investment opportunities.

Still, he earned a small fortune, so he had obviously played the game right.

Whilst she, Rosie, hadn't started playing it at all.

'With Christmas just three weeks away...' Candice shifted and Rosie looked at her sister with narrowed eyes, smelling a conversation ahead that she would not want to have.

'Don't worry, I'll make sure the chalet is in tip-top shape for the family invasion. You know how much I love the whole decorating thing. Plus, I'll make sure there are lots of chocolates hanging on the branches of the tree for Toby and Jess.'

'There has been a slight change of plan. The snow is so magnificent at the moment that everyone's coming over a little earlier than originally planned.'

'Earlier than planned?'

'Tomorrow, as it happens. I'm the advanced warning party, so to speak. I know you and I had planned a couple of girly days together but you know Mum and Dad...they can't resist the slopes and the atmosphere here at Christmas. And there's something else,' Candice said in a rush. 'They're thinking of asking the Ashley-Talbots over for a long weekend. Bertie too. He's something or other in the City and doing quite well, I hear. They think it might be nice for you two to...er... get to know one another...'

'No.'

'It's just a thought, Rosie. Nothing's confirmed. He's always had that crush on you, you know. It might be nice!'

'Absolutely not, Candice.'

'Mum and Dad just thought that there's no harm in actually meeting someone a little less...*unorthodox.*'

'When you say that you're the advance warning party—' Rosie narrowed suspicious eyes '—does that actually mean that you've been sent to start preparing me for lots of lectures on getting my house in order, starting with dating Robert Ashley-Talbot? Well, no way will I be getting involved with him! He's...he's the most *boring* guy I've ever met!'

'You can't say that! You might find that you actually enjoy the company of someone who has a *steady job*, Rosie! Emily and I both happen to agree with Mum and Dad! Give me *one* good reason, Rosie-Boo, why you won't at least give it a go. If you find that you really don't like Bertie, then that's fair enough, but you haven't seen him in *years.*'

'A year and a half, and he can't have changed that much.' Nerdy, prominent Adam's apple, thick-rimmed glasses and a way of getting onto a really dull topic of conversation and then bedding down for the duration.

Rosie looked down. Down to the lively buzz of excited guests, down to the glittering Christmas tree, down to the clutch of leather chairs in the foyer, where a group of three people was gathering some papers, shaking hands, clearly about to leave.

'And—' she turned her clear blue-eyed gaze back to her sister '—I wasn't going to say anything but…but… I'm just not in a good place for meeting Bertie, Diss. Or *anyone,* for that matter.'

On her lap, she crossed her fingers and told herself that this was a perfectly sensible way out of a situation that would turn Christmas into a nightmare. She didn't want Bertie coming over. She didn't want to have to face the full force of her family gently trying to propel her to a destination she didn't want to go because they were concerned about her.

She leaned forward. 'I've had my heart broken while I've been out here.'

'What on earth are you talking about, Rosie?'

'You say that I never go for the right kind of guy? Well, I did. I fell for one of the guests here. A businessman. As reliable and as stable as…as…the day is long. He was everything you and Ems and Mum and Dad would have wanted for me, which just goes to show that those types just aren't for girls like me. I bore them in the end. It was just a holiday fling but I guess I got more wrapped up in him than I thought I would.'

'I'm not sure I believe you,' Candice said, eyebrows raised. 'It's very odd that this is the first I'm hearing of this and we've been sitting here for what…an hour? What a co-incidence.'

'I wasn't going to mention it but I felt I had to when you told me that Mum and Dad were thinking of asking Robert and his parents over for the weekend. I'm just a little shaken up, that's all. I know I've dated the wrong sorts but I really felt that this guy might be the one. I went into it with my eyes wide open and I was hurt. So… I just need a bit of time out to lick my wounds.'

'And where is this mysterious disappearing man right now?' But her voice was hesitant, on the cusp of believing.

'As a matter of fact…'

And there was that group of three again. She recognised the elderly couple—Bob and Margaret something-or-other. She had given them both a lesson, filling in for their usual instructor who had called in sick when Rosie knew for a fact he had been suffering from a hangover. They had said were there to try and learn to ski because, although they were in their late sixties, they believed that old dogs could be taught new tricks and, since their daughter loved her skiing, they were up for giving it a try. They were going to be retiring. Selling up. A nice young man, Matteo, would be coming in for a flying visit to do the deal. Exciting times.

With his back to her as he shook hands with the older man, Matteo—or the man she assumed was Matteo, because who else could it possibly be?—was just the candidate for the role of businessman heartbreaker. There was no way she intended to spend her Christmas dodging Bertie, and a broken heart was the only excuse she could find that might save her from that dreadful possibility.

'There he is. Matteo. With that couple about to leave. He's here on business with them. He doesn't know that I'm up here looking down at him. Thinks I'm out on the slopes giving a lesson. He's probably completely forgotten about my existence already.'

She looked at her sister who stared down to the group of three, eyes narrowed.

'*That* creep was the guy who hurt you?'

Rosie mumbled something inarticulate,

meant to convey an affirmative reply without going into further detail. Not a liar by nature, she was guiltily aware that she was blackening a perfect stranger's character with her little white lie.

Distracted, what happened next took her by surprise. It was so out of keeping with her cool, collected, elegant blonde sister. Candice was *always* so controlled! But here she was now, angrily rising to her feet, hands slapping down on the table, and then she was hurtling between tables, feet flying at a pace while… Rosie watched, mouth open, horror slowly dawning because she knew that this was not going to end well for her…

She would have to stop her sister before things went any further. She didn't waste time thinking about it. She leapt up and followed in hot pursuit.

For once, Matteo Moretti wasn't looking at his watch. He usually did. The end of a deal always awakened a restlessness inside him, an impatience to move on to the next thing. True, the signatures on the dotted line were technically not there yet, but that was a formality. Hands had been shaken and, as soon as the horror of the Christmas season was over and done with, the lawyers would be summoned and the finishing touches put to a purchase that meant a great deal to him.

Bob and Margaret Taylor, the most unlikely of clients, were beaming up at him. Bob, yet again, was congratulating him in his bluff, Yorkshire accent for getting past the post.

'Land's worth a bob or two.' He slapped Matteo's arm and winked. 'Can't tell you how many wanted to get their greedy paws on it but you're the first person the missus and I feel we can trust to do the right thing.'

'Honoured that you think that,' Matteo responded with sincerity.

He'd been here at this eye-wateringly pricey resort for the past three days, wooing Bob and his wife. A different type of approach for a very different type of deal.

Around him, Yuletide merriment had been a constant backdrop, getting on his nerves, reminding him that it was high time he did what he always did every single Christmas—escape. Escape to his villa on the outskirts of Venice, which was a mere couple of hours from here.

He worked in London and had a penthouse apartment there, indeed lived most of his life there, but his elegant, yellow-stone villa here in Italy was his bolt-hole and the only place where he felt perfectly at peace. Every year he removed himself from the canned carols, the ridiculous Santa lookalikes ringing bells outside supermarkets and the pounding of crowds on pavements, frantically hunting down presents, wrapping paper, Christmas decorations and all the paraphernalia that seemed to arrive earlier and earlier in the shops with every passing year.

Two weeks away from it all, isolated in his sprawling manor with two trusted employees to cook and clean for him while he worked. God bless broadband and the Internet. It enabled him to avoid the chaos of the festive season while still keeping on top of each and every detail of what was happening in his various offices across the globe. He might live in England but he was Italian and this bolt-hole in Italy reminded him of his heritage and everything that went with it. He threw money at his PA, told her to do as she wished when it came to entertaining the troops at various office Christmas parties and he disappeared.

'Just a couple more "i"s to dot and a couple more "t"s to cross and it's yours, lad, and we couldn't be happier.'

Intensely private and remote, Matteo felt the twist of something highly emotional swell inside him because this was the one and only deal he had ever done that had real personal significance. His background, his childhood—in a way the very reason he was where he was now—all lay in that land he was on the verge of buying and the halfway house within it. It was a place of retreat for foster kids, an escape where they could feel what it was like to be in the open countryside, with nature all around them. Horses to ride, quiet, secret places to go and just *be,* chickens to feed and eggs to collect. An idyll.

So many years ago, but a fortnight spent there, when he had been just ten and about to go off the rails in a big way, had done something to him, had given him something to hold onto. He had found an anchor in a restless, rudderless existence and had somehow held onto that. Bob and Margaret hadn't been in charge at the time. They had come later, and of course he'd kept that connection to the place to himself, as he kept everything of a personal nature to himself. But with ownership of that special place within his grasp… Yes, he felt strangely emotional.

Shaking Bob's hand as they made plans for their final meeting, Matteo was ill prepared for what happened next.

A scene.

A blonde woman bearing down on them

from nowhere. The high pitch of her voice was as piercing as the scrape of fingernails on a blackboard. Heads spun round, mouths opened and closed and there was a flurry of activity as stunned hotel employees and guests alike gasped and wondered what was going on.

For a split second, Matteo was utterly lost for words. Next to him, Bob and Margaret were also stunned into immobility.

'Who do you think you are... Matteo whoever you are...? How *dare* you mess with Rosie? People like you should be strung up! And I guess you're going to run away and leave her all broken-hearted. And I bet you won't even look back. You have no morals at *all*! She's been hurt too many times!'

'Are you talking *to me*?'

'Who else could I be talking to? Is your name Matteo?'

'Yes, but there seems to have been some kind of misunderstanding...'

Matteo, already on the back foot, peered around the tall blonde to see a shorter, plump girl, wearing an expression of dismay, borderline panic and acute embarrassment.

For a few seconds, he was utterly nonplussed. She was staring directly at him and she had the bluest eyes he had ever seen. Her hair was vanilla-blonde, a tangle of unruly curls framing a heart-shaped face that was, just at the moment, suffused with colour. Her mouth was a perfect bow shape and her skin was satiny smooth.

Words failed him. He stared. He registered that she was calling his name and then, somehow taking advantage of that moment of weird disorientation he had experienced at seeing her, he realised she was leading him away from the others with a sharp tug on his arm.

'Please, please, *please*...' Rosie was whispering, simultaneously tiptoeing and tugging him down so that she could whisper into his ear, 'Could you just play along with this for the moment? I'll explain in a bit. I'm really, *really* sorry, but all you have to do is...'

Is what? Matteo thought. Through the confusion of his thoughts, he felt her small, delicate hands clutch at his arm. She was so much smaller than Matteo, his tall form and muscular body towering over her.

'Who the hell are *you*?' Matteo kept his voice low, a whispered conversation that he knew looked a lot more intimate than it was. He was thinking fast but was disconcerted by the softness of her body and the sweet, floral scent of her hair. She was much shorter than him and her reaching up to him somehow emphasised the fullness of her breasts, pushing against her jumper, just brushing against him.

'Rosie. Sorry. Sorry, sorry, sorry. I had no idea my sister would rush down here like a tornado…'

'This isn't what I expected from you, son. You know how traditional I am when it comes to treating other people the way you would want to be treated yourself.' This from behind him—Bob's voice, thick with disappointment.

How the hell did the woman know his name? And who was she anyway? His head was clearing and one thing was certain—the ramifications of what was going on were becoming patently obvious.

No deal.

Lengthy unravelling of this mess was going to take time and time was not on his side. Bob was making noises under his breath, wondering whether he hadn't made a dreadful mistake, while his wife was trying to be the voice of reason. The deal was disappearing into the ether. He had no idea who was the woman imploring his help. His assumption was it was some kind of set-up somehow to extract money from him. He was made of money. Public accusations of some kind? Blackmail?

Press somewhere waiting in the wings, cameras at the ready?

His levels of anger bordered on volcanic. Of key importance was to take this scene away from Bob and his wife and sort out the consequences later. Damage limitation was essential. He wanted this deal and he was going to do whatever it took to seal it.

And the only thing he could think of doing right now was to follow the lead of the pink-faced girl still looking at him and play along, much as he didn't want to.

He smiled and Rosie went a shade pinker.

'Rosie,' he murmured, spinning her round and edging them both back to the group, who had fallen silent during their whispered *tête-à-tête*, including the screeching sister. 'You know we talked about this…'

He looked at Bob and Margaret with a self-deprecating smile and anchored the fiery little blonde closer to him so that she was nestled against his side. 'She's gone off the rails because she thinks I'm going to be one of those fly-by-night guys…' He shook his head, leant down and brushed his mouth against her cheek. 'How can I convince you, my darling, that this isn't just a fling for me?'

Rosie looked at him. Her skin burned where he had brushed it with his mouth. His arm, hooked around her waist, was doing all sorts of things to her body, making her squirm.

In the heat of the moment, she hadn't quite appreciated just how stunning the guy was. Raven-black hair, bronzed skin and eyes as dark as midnight. She knew that she was breathing quickly, just as she knew that she wasn't thinking straight. She was conscious of her femininity in ways she hadn't thought possible.

'Um…'

'This feels like the start of something big, Bob,' Matteo said in a darkly persuasive voice. 'I would have mentioned it to you but I didn't want to jinx it.'

'So romantic,' Margaret was saying with approval.

'Isn't it?' Matteo commented neutrally. He tightened his hand on Rosie's waist and gave her the tiniest of squeezes, nudging her ever closer, thigh against thigh, his arm resting just below her breast now.

Rosie felt the tightening of her nipples. She had no intention of catching her sister's eye but she could feel Candice looking at the pair of them and heaven only knew what was going through her head. Candice was astute but it had to be said that this dark stranger, dragged into a charade not of his making, was doing a fine job of pulling it off and her only question was *why*?

'You should head back to your hotel.' Matteo's primary objective at this point was to put distance between Bob, Margaret and the combustible situation unfolding in front of them. 'Long day tomorrow finalising our deal.'

'You're getting a good man in this one,' Bob said warmly, moving in to shake Rosie's hand. 'Glad everything's sorted, lad. Misunderstandings can get out of control! Nice to see you've got the makings of a family man within you. A good woman is always the making of any man.' He chuckled and gave his wife a hug.

Matteo thought it best to speed things along. He had no idea what was going on but the threat of it all blowing up was a distinct possibility and one he intended to divert with everything at his disposal. He mentally bid a temporary farewell to his Venetian villa that was waiting for him the following evening. It wasn't going to happen.

'So they say,' he murmured as he thought ahead to how he intended to squash whatever machinations were afoot. 'Comprehensively' was the word that sprang to mind.

'Hope we get to spend some time with the two of you before we head back to Yorkshire. Family is everything, like I say, and I wouldn't mind raising a glass or two to celebrate young love.'

Matteo murmured, nodded, half-smiled, brushed his lips against Rosie's hair… He exerted every ounce of charm to smooth over the sudden, alarming pot holes that had surfaced on the very smooth road. He walked them to the glass door, where they were waiting to be met, the little blonde still by his side because question time was about to begin.

Rosie watched with mounting dread as Matteo disposed of her sister with ruthless speed. He was the essence of charm, even though his hand on her waist carried the hint of a threat that sent shivers racing up and down her spine. She could hardly blame him. She listened in mutely as he smoothed over Candice's doubts, laying it on thick until Candice was smiling and telling him how relieved she was that things were back on track, apologising for the fuss and then, somehow, laughingly blaming *Rosie* for having given her the wrong impression.

Rosie couldn't believe the way events had

transpired. Who knew that her five-foot-ten, ice-queen sister could let rip with such uncharacteristic drama? Candice was the one who flinched if someone raised their voice slightly too loudly in a restaurant. She moaned about people shouting into their mobile phones in public! She'd once told Emily off, when they had just been kids, for laughing too much.

Candice out of the way, Matteo dropped his hand, stood back and surveyed the blonde coldly.

'So,' he said flatly, 'Let's find somewhere nice and cosy and private and have a little chat, shall we?'

Rosie quailed. The man was sexy, dangerous…and from the expression on his face in the presence of his quarry.

'I'm really sorry, I—I know how this must look…' she stammered, only dimly aware that he was leading her out of the crowded foyer. She found she couldn't quite meet those wintry eyes.

'Do you, now?' Matteo purred.

Where was he taking her? She cast a desperate backward glance behind her, back down to the marbled foyer with the tall Christmas tree. The low buzz of curious voices that had greeted the little scene earlier had died down but there would still be curious eyes looking to see whether it might kick off again.

'Where are we going?'

'Somewhere private,' Matteo murmured, voice as smooth as silk and as razor-sharp as a knife, 'Where we can have our cosy little chat.'

'I've already apologised...' Her legs, however, were obeying his command. She stood up and began walking alongside him, hyper-aware of his presence. There was a leashed power to the guy that made her quiver with a combination of apprehension, downright fear and a weird sort of breathless excitement that stemmed from a place she couldn't quite put her finger on.

He wasn't saying a word and seemed un-aware of the cluster of well-heeled people around him that parted to allow him passage as if in the presence of royalty.

It was extraordinary.

She had no idea where they were going but eventually they reached a door which he slid open, standing back to allow her to brush past him.

She'd never been into this particular inner sanctum, even though she had been com-ing to this very resort with her parents for as long as she could remember, before they'd bought their own chalet just a bit further up the slopes.

It was a large, square room, richly panelled, with a gleaming wooden floor that was largely covered by an expanse of expensive, silk Persian rug. A cluster of deep, comfortable sofas was positioned here and there and a long bar extended along the back of one panelled wall. Rosie assumed this was the chill-out area for the senior management who ran the resort, somewhere where they could relax and unwind, away from the clamour of what might be going on outside.

She stared around her and, when she settled her eyes back on Matteo, it was to find that he had made himself at home and poured a whisky for himself. Needless to say, there was no offer of any form of refreshment for her.

'Okay,' Rosie began. 'I know what you're going to say and I'm sorry.'

'First, you have no idea what I'm going to say, and secondly, if you're sorry now, then you're going to be a whole lot sorrier when I'm through with you and your accomplice.'

'Accomplice?' She gazed at him, bewildered, and then wished she hadn't because he seemed to have the most peculiar effect on her. He made her feel as though the room was beginning to spin and if she didn't sit down fast she would topple to the ground in an undignified heap.

'The blonde with a voice that could shatter glass. Sit.'

A voice that could shatter glass? That was a first when it came to a description of her sister. Of either of her sisters, for that matter. Both were tall, sophisticated and impossibly beautiful in an ice-queen kind of way. Whereas she was… Rosie: short, way too plump because of the siren call of chocolate and all things sweet, with shoulder-length blonde hair that refused to be tamed, breasts far too abundant to be fashionable…

She recalled the heat of his hand so close to her breast and shivered.

Conscious of each and every one of those downsides, and aware of those cool, cool eyes on her, she haltingly headed for the closest chair and dropped into it, little knowing what was coming but all too ready to take the blame.

'If that little scene was some half-baked attempt to screw money out of me then you messed with the wrong guy,' he said flatly. He didn't raise his voice or move a muscle but for all that the single sentence was imbued with threat and Rosie shivered and licked her lips.

'I came here to do a deal that means a great deal to me,' he continued, in the same deathly subdued, almost conversational tone. 'Which is why I played along with whatever game you fancied you'd set in motion. I'm going to play along just until my deal is done, and then, let's just say you'll understand the meaning of regret.'

'You can't threaten me,' Rosie objected weakly. 'And that woman was my sister, not an accomplice!'

'Can't threaten you? No, you've got that wrong, I'm afraid. Here's the thing, whoever the hell you are—whatever scheme you and your sister or whoever she was have concocted, you can bury it, because there's no money at the end of this particular rainbow.'

'Money?'

'Did you really think that you would create a public scene to grab my attention, hurl baseless accusations against me to grab the *public's* attention and then somehow manoeuvre me into a place where I would part with hard cash to shut the pair of you up?'

'I have no idea what you're talking about.'

'Don't play games with me, miss!'

'I'm *not* playing games! I honestly have no idea what you're getting at! Are you saying that you think my sister and I are out to get money from you? Why would we want to do that?'

Matteo clicked his tongue with blatant incredulity, reached into his pocket and extracted a card from his wallet, which he tossed onto her lap. Then he sat back and crossed his legs.

'How *rude*!' Rosie exploded, her face bright red. 'Is this how you treat women? How dare you just…just fling something at me?'

'Spare me the self-righteous outrage,' he returned smoothly. 'Why don't you have a look at the card?'

Still fuming, Rosie looked at the card, which had just a name on it and three telephone numbers. She politely reached forward to return it.

'I'm sorry but this doesn't mean anything to me. Well, I guess it's your name. Matteo Moretti.' She sighed. He'd taken the card back and was obviously waiting for her to expand. His expression was unreadable and she got the impression that this was a man who knew how to conceal what was in his head and that it was something he was accustomed to doing. He emanated a certain amount of menace but she wondered whether that hint of menace wasn't amplified by the fact that she was just so *conscious* of him in a way she had never been conscious of any man in her life before.

Suddenly very much aware of her physical shortcomings, she fidgeted in the chair and tried to get herself into a suitably more elevated, commanding position.

'I suppose you're someone important, which is why you think I should recognise your name, but I don't know who's who in the world of business. You must be rich, because you think that I'm some kind of master criminal who wants your money, but you're wrong.'

'Your sister knew my name,' Matteo said bluntly. 'Care to explain?'

'Her name is Candice.'

'Irrelevant. Just answer my question. Time is money.'

Sinfully good-looking he might be but Rosie was beginning to think that he was the most odious guy she had ever encountered. Rude didn't begin to cover it.

'I teach skiing here,' she said stiffly. 'For the season. I happened to meet your…your friends on the slopes. Pierre was supposed to be giving them a lesson but he went out last night with his girlfriend and he didn't show up for—'

'Get to the point!'

'I'm getting there! Bob and Margaret told me that they were here mixing business with pleasure. They told me your name—Matteo. They said you never left the hotel, then they laughed and said that if they didn't get to grips with skiing then you were to blame because they were too busy feeling guilty about you being cooped up inside to concentrate on getting their feet in the right place. Obviously I didn't know it was *you* at the time, but that's how I happened to know your name. It was just coincidence that you happened to be where you were when…'

When all hell broke loose.

Matteo gritted his teeth. 'How much more tortured can this explanation get? I feel as though I'm being made to sample a vision of hell. Are you ever going to get to the point or do I have to bring the police in to question you?'

'Police? How *dare* you?' She glared at him and he stared back at her without batting an eyelid.

'Just. Get. To. The. Point.'

'Okay, here's the point!' Rosie snapped, leaning forward and gripping the sides of her chair tightly. 'I had to pretend that I had broken up with someone, because I didn't want to be condemned to seeing Bertie over

Christmas, and I spotted you down there in
the foyer with Bob and Margaret and I… I…
figured that you were the businessman called
Matteo so I lied and told my sister that I'd
been seeing you! Is that enough of an explanation for you? I'm really sorry but you were
the fall guy!'

CHAPTER TWO

THEIR EYES MET. Matteo was beginning to feel a little unsteady. He had never before heard such a garbled non-explanation from anyone in response to any question he had ever posed in his life. Her mouth was parted and she was leaning forward, her body language speaking of an urgency for him to believe what she was saying.

The woman was distracting.

It wasn't just the breathless, convoluted workings of her brain which he was finding extraordinarily difficult to deal with. It was *her,* the entire package. The second he had laid eyes on her, something inside him had kick-started and now…staring back into her impossibly turquoise eyes…

He shifted, frowning. There was enough on his plate without losing focus over this nonsense. His eyes roved over her flushed face, subliminally appreciating the satin smoothness of her skin and the juicy fullness of her lips. As he watched, her tongue flicked out, nervously licking her upper lip, and his whole body jack-knifed in sudden, heated response.

A libido which had been dormant for the past six months surged into life with shocking force. He gritted his teeth together but he had to shift position because his erection was rock-hard, pulsing against the zipper of his trousers.

Was she leaning forward like that on purpose? Making sure that those lush, heavy breasts were on tempting show, begging to be fondled?

Matteo had a very particular type of woman. Very tall, very slim and very brunette. He went for the career woman, the woman who challenged him intellectually. He liked the back and forth of informed conversation about politics and the economy. He liked them cool, confident and as driven as he was. He'd fought hard for his place in the world and he appreciated a woman who had battled against the odds as well. An ambitious woman with a career of her own was also not a needy woman, and he disliked needy women. He didn't want anyone needing him. He operated solo and that was the way he liked it.

So why was he staring at this woman in front of him with the rapt attention of a horny teenager? She was breathy and ultra-feminine and didn't strike him as the sort who would be winning awards for her thoughts on world finance. She was the antithesis of what he sought in any woman.

Furious with his lack of self-control, he leapt to his feet to prowl through the room, at the same time finishing the glass of whisky he had poured, tempted to help himself to another but resisting the urge.

He had to remove his eyes from the sexy woman on the chair but, when he finally glanced at her again, it was to find that he was still in the grip of whatever ludicrous spell she had temporarily cast on him.

He positioned himself in front of her and then leant down, gripping either side of the chair, caging her in so that she instinctively drew back.

Her breathing was fast and shallow, her breasts heaving.

'Not going to work,' he growled.

'What are you talking about?' Rosie whispered. 'I've tried to explain what happened.'

'You expect me to believe that I was just some random target? That you really have no idea as to the reach of my power? And, if that's the case, why are you coming on to me?'

Rosie's mouth fell open and she stared.

'I beg your pardon?'

'Don't think that you're going to get me into any sort of compromising situation! I wasn't born yesterday. That garbled nonsense about dragging me into this situation to avoid a guy—unbelievable.'

'Compromising situation?'

'You're a sexy woman but I'm not a fool.' Matteo gritted his teeth, controlling his hands with extreme difficulty, because what he desperately wanted to do was take what was obviously on offer, starting with those luscious lips and moving on to the even more luscious breasts.

'You're telling me that *I'm sexy*?'

'And advertising it isn't going to work. Where's your sister? Lurking behind the door? Ready to take an incriminating photo, perhaps?' He pushed himself away from the chair but his body was still on fire as he strolled through the room, purposefully maintaining distance between them.

Eventually, he sat down. He was still hard, still turned on.

'I can't believe you'd imagine that I was coming onto you,' Rosie said faintly. The thought alone was enough to suffuse her with colour.

Her? She was the one who had drawn the short straw when it came to looks. Her sisters had always been the ones to turn heads. She, Rosie, had been the girl the boys enjoyed hanging out with. She self-consciously folded her arms over her breasts and then realised that, in doing so, she had simply drawn attention to them.

She wondered whether that would lead to another crazy accusation that she was trying to come on to him. Her skin prickled. He had called her *sexy* and she didn't think that he'd been kidding.

'And it wasn't garbled nonsense,' she belatedly continued. 'If you'd just listen! My family…' Her voice was staccato with suppressed nerves. 'Well, you've met Candice, my sister. They've been a bit concerned about me…they think I need to settle down, find a job, a life partner…'

'A *life partner*?'

'Yes.' She flushed. Why had she launched into this brutally honest explanation? Why hadn't she skimmed over the details? The way he was looking at her, frowning in silence with his head tilted to one side, was bringing her out in goose bumps. She should have left him puzzled about the nonsensical reason for her behaviour because now she would have to confess that the last thing she was was *sexy*. *Sexy* women didn't have their entire protective family twitching with concern about their life choices.

'How old are you?'

'Twenty-three.'

'Let's suspend disbelief for the moment and go along with your story: why are you supposed to have a *life partner* at the age of twenty-three?'

Matteo realised, with frustration, that the woman was doing it again. Distracting him. He raked his fingers through his hair and reminded himself that this was the woman who had probably scuppered his deal, the one deal that mattered even though he had nothing to gain financially from it.

She looked as pure as the driven snow but he knew better than to trust the way people looked. Scratch the surface and there was usual a healthy store of avarice and general unpleasantness to be found.

She was gazing at him with those incredible aquamarine eyes.

Matteo was beginning to think that she wasn't the Machiavellian character he had first assumed, working in cahoots with a partner in crime. For once, his cynicism might be misplaced. He wasn't going to give up the notion willingly, but...he was getting there.

Nor was he convinced that she had been trying to come on to him, he grudgingly conceded. She was either an actress of Oscar winning standard or her shock at the accusation had been genuine.

He was so accustomed to women making a play for him, that the idea of one actively horrified at the thought of it was as novel as discovering a fish riding a bike in the centre of Hyde Park.

No ulterior motive, which just left her explanation that she had started an ill-thought-out act of impulse to escape some guy's advances.

This time, when he looked at her, it was with lazy interest. He was thirty-two years old but his palate was lamentably jaded. This slice of novelty was strangely compelling.

'Aren't you a little young to be told that you need to start thinking about settling down?' He shifted, making a concerted effort not to give in to the urge to stare at her fabulous body. 'And, conversely, a little old for your family to be the ones giving the lectures?'

Rosie bristled. 'They care about me. Not that that's any of your business.'

'Everything is my business when, thanks to you, the deal I've been nurturing for the past eight months will probably come to nothing. Whether what you and your sister did was a deliberate ruse or not, the upshot remains the same.'

'Bob and Margaret seem very reasonable people, not the sort to jeopardise whatever agreement you reached with them because of a scene in a hotel lobby.' Rosie flushed as her guilty conscience ate away at her. She couldn't understand why he needed any deal so badly when it was obvious that he was made of money. Her parents were rich but she suspected that this guy was in a different league altogether.

'Bob and Margaret are deeply traditional people,' Matteo informed her coolly. 'Church goers with an extremely healthy respect for the family unit, as you may have gathered. My integrity has been paramount to winning their trust.'

'I'm really and truly sorry. I had no idea that my sister would fly down there and let rip. It's not like her at all. She *never* makes a fuss. She's probably at the chalet right now broadcasting our relationship to the entire family.'

'The chalet?'

'My parents own a chalet about fifteen minutes from here.' She stared off into the distance and wondered what the next step was going to be.

Her gaze slid over to where Matteo was still staring at her, his loose-limbed body relaxed and her heart picked up speed. He was so perfect...so stupendously good-looking.

'You still haven't properly explained what went on down there,' Matteo prompted, his voice clipped. 'Now Cupid has supposedly targeted us, you might as well fill me in on this guy you don't want to meet and why you're having to in the first place. I didn't ask for this but it's landed on my lap and I'm going to have to make the best of it. I'll need some personal details about you.'

Rosie looked at him and then found that she couldn't stop looking and, when she looked, her brain went into overdrive and she started thinking about the way his mouth had felt against her cheek.

'I...well...as I mentioned, my family think it's time for me to start settling down—and please don't tell me that I'm too old to have my sisters and my parents fussing around me. I know that. Fact is, Candice came over to warn me that they were thinking of inviting some family friends to the chalet over Christmas.' She grimaced. 'Bertie is their son.'

'And?' Matteo tilted his head and looked at her with raised eyebrows. 'You don't like him? Ex-lover? Bad break-up? Where are we going with this one?'

'You're very rude, aren't you?' She scowled and then, without warning, he smiled at her and all that sexiness was thrown into such stark focus that she was temporarily shocked into silence.

The harsh beauty of his face was no longer forbidding. All of a sudden, Rosie glimpsed at what true sexiness in a guy was all about and in an instant every boyfriend she had ever had faded into insignificance. She had gone out with silly little boys. The glorious specimen sprawled in front of her was just the opposite. He was all man, an alpha male in the prime of his life. She felt faint.

'No one has ever said that to me before,' Matteo drawled. 'Should I be irritated, bemused or intrigued?'

Rosie squirmed. She wasn't sure how to answer that question or whether he even expected an answer. She felt hot and bothered, as if she was coming down with something.

'My parents think that Bertie and I might be a good match and I guess...' She hesitated.

'I acted without thinking. Candice was sitting across from me, ruining my entire Christmas. I just looked down and spotted Bob and Margaret and the guy they said they'd been doing business with, and I knew that you were all leaving, so I...told my sister that I couldn't possibly face Bertie because I'd been having a fling with you, which hadn't worked out and I was all broken up. It seemed safe. You were going and there was no way I thought she was ever going to...do what she ended up doing.'

Hearing it spoken out loud, Rosie couldn't imagine why she had done what she had. Why hadn't she just stood her ground and refused?

She knew why. Because it had always been her nature to follow the path of least resistance and that had evolved into her just going with the flow.

'I should have just told Candice that if Bertie was going to be on the scene then I would make sure not to be there. I should have had a bit more will power. Instead, I acted on impulse, and I'm sorry.'

'I'm getting the picture of someone who lets her family run her life for her. Am I right?'

'Is there anything I can do to make it up to you?'

'You shouldn't make offers like that,' Matteo murmured. 'A guy could get all the wrong ideas.'

Heat coursed through her body, a slow burn from the inside out. Her breasts ached and her nipples, straining against her bra, felt ultra-sensitive, tingling. She imagined the pads of his fingers rubbing them and her breathing became shallow and laboured. She had no experience when it came to this kind of sophisticated, lazy flirting. If that was even what it was. All she could do was stare at him while her mind continued to play with all sorts of graphic, contraband images.

What on earth was wrong with her?

This guy reeked of danger and yet the pull she felt was overpowering.

'So, now that we're an item, what happens next?'

'I…well…'

'In the thick of this relationship, our hot, two-week clandestine fling, where were we supposed to be meeting? My room at the hotel? Your parents' chalet? Neither of the above? It's a mystery that Bob and Margaret didn't jump in with a string of questions about our so-called affair, bearing in mind most of my time over the past few days has been spent with them working on finishing touches to my deal.'

'How am I supposed to know?' Rosie retorted truthfully. 'I didn't stop to think things through.'

Impulse on that scale was unheard of in Matteo's world and it was strangely refreshing to glimpse a life where variables were given a chance to survive. Not for him, and yet... 'Well, we're going to have to come up with some sort of plausible story or else the whole thing falls apart, and I'm not about to let that happen.'

'Because of this deal you're working on?'

'I just need to get past the finishing line.'

'Why?'

'Come again?'

'Why would a deal mean so much to you that you would go along with this charade instead of just calling me out? I mean, you seem to have enough money...'

'You've lived a life of comfort,' Matteo said coolly. 'From that vantage point, it's easy to come out with platitudes about not needing money or having enough of it. Tell me, have you ever told anyone that the best things in life are free? Take it from me, they seldom are. Now, back to my question—what happens next? Your sister is staying with you.

Having witnessed our show of love, presumably she expects nothing less than a formal meeting with the man who's head over heels in love with you?'

Rosie's brain was only just beginning to move on from what he had said about her attitude towards money. She was mortified to realise that he was right. She'd led a charmed life and it was easy to take all that for granted when you knew that it would always be there. For all her free-spirited travelling, she would never have fallen very far, because there would always have been a cushion waiting for her.

'She's probably curious,' Rosie admitted.

'And the over-protective family? Will the grape vine be buzzing with news of our whirlwind romance?'

Rosie shot him a sheepish smile and pushed some tangled blonde curls off her face.

'"Buzzing" might be an understatement,' she confessed.

'But at least the ex-lover won't be on the scene now you're spoken for.' He'd felt it again. A charge of electricity, powerful and disorientating. Primal. She represented everything he steered clear of when it came to women, and yet she was uniquely appealing and he had no idea from where the appeal stemmed.

'Bertie was never an ex,' Rosie was obliged to point out. 'Never even came close! Our families have known each other for ages and, somewhere along the line, he got it into his head that he wanted to ask me out on a date. I was seventeen at the time. I've never fancied him but now he's a big shot in the City somewhere and everyone thinks he could be a suitable match.' She rolled her eyes.

Matteo didn't say anything. His dark eyes were lazy and thoughtful. 'So I'll be meeting the family,' he murmured.

'You don't have to. I could tell them that you've been called away on business. Candice has met you. She'll understand.'

'Why will she understand?'

'Because…' Rosie thought that, for someone as forbidding as he was, it was oddly easy to talk to him. 'Because she has two children now, but before that she was a successful lawyer, so she understands the demands of work. She'll get it if you pay a flying visit and then disappear.'

Rosie frowned and sat forward. 'That would work,' she said slowly. 'If you disappear, then there won't be the complication of your meeting my parents and the rest of the family. That way, I can gradually warn them that the big romance isn't actually going as planned. These things happen,' she thought aloud. 'People meet and think that they've fallen in love but it turns out to be a mistake.'

'And naturally,' Matteo said soothingly, 'That's exactly what will happen but, for the moment, that solution is off the cards.'

'Why?'

'Because my deal hasn't been finalised. Bob and Margaret are here for another week. Skiing, having fun and making sure the last details of my purchase are drawn up and inspected via email by their lawyers in London. Until signatures are on the dotted line, we're in love and thinking of building a future together. Once everything's signed, sealed and delivered, then the hasty unravelling of our relationship can begin.' He gave an elegant shrug which implied that that was the way forward and there was nothing she could do about it, whether she wanted to or not.

'It'll be harder on my parents if they actually meet you face to face.'

'Tough.' Matteo didn't bother beating about the bush. 'I didn't ask for this.'

His dark eyes scoured her face. He could read the tension and anxiety there, and of course she had a point. She clearly came from a tight-knit family unit. The less they were hurt by her behaviour, the better, but as far as he was concerned that was not his problem. Matteo didn't allow sentiment to rule his life. It simply wasn't in his nature. He had managed to remain focused, to stay on course with his life—unlike many of the kids he had grown up with, who had ended up either in jail or six feet under. That said, a life spent in foster care had toughened him. He had known what it meant to have nothing, to be a face and a name in a system and not much more. He had climbed out of that place and forged his way in the world.

That brief spell of respite at the place he was in the process of buying had shown him that there were alternatives in life. He had held onto that vision and it had seen him through.

He had realised that the only way to escape the predictability of becoming one of the victims of the Social Services system was to educate himself and he had applied himself to the task with monumental dedication. By the time he had hit Cambridge University, he had been an intellectual force to contend with.

He'd known more than his tutors. His aptitude for mathematics was prodigious. He'd been head-hunted by a newly formed investment bank and had swiftly risen to the top before breaking free to become something of a shooting star in the financial firmament. Money had given him the opportunity to diversify. It had allowed him to get whatever he wanted at the snap of a finger. Money had been his passport to freedom and freedom had been his only goal for his entire adult life.

Money had also jaded his palate, made life predictable. Being able to have whatever and whomever you wanted, he had reflected time and again, did not necessarily guarantee excitement.

He hadn't had a woman in months and he hadn't been tempted.

Now here he was and, in that instant, Matteo decided that he was going to go with the flow and make the best of the situation into which he had been catapulted. Moreover, he was going to enjoy the experience.

'I have a suite here, at this hotel,' he mused. 'Bob and Margaret are at another location, further down the slopes. If I'm the new man in your life, then I'll be expected to be at your parents' chalet with you, I presume?'

'Wait. What? Now, hang on just a minute...'

'It's hardly likely that we're in the thick of a stormy, passionate affair and I'm bedding down on my own in a hotel room while you're miles away in a chalet somewhere with nothing but the telly and a good book for company. Is it?'

'Well, no. but…'

'But?'

'But this isn't a normal situation, is it? I mean, we're not actually involved with one another, are we?'

'You need to follow the plot line here,' Matteo imparted kindly. 'There will be people we will need to convince and no one, not even traditional and church-going Bob and Margaret, will be persuaded that this is the affair of a lifetime if we're crossing paths off and on.'

'Stop being patronising,' Rosie said absently. What did he mean by being at the chalet with her? Sharing a bedroom? She paled at the thought because suddenly her little white lie had taken on a life of its own and was galloping away at speed.

Matteo burst out laughing and she focused on his handsome face and glared.

'I hadn't banked on this,' she said tightly. 'You may find the whole thing hilarious but I don't.'

'I don't find anything hilarious about this situation,' Matteo shot back and, she thought for the millionth time, there was no need for him to remind her that she had brought this mess on herself. 'But here we are. I'm going to move into your parents' chalet today.'

'Candice will know that you haven't been living with me,' Rosie pointed out.

'How?'

'There would be signs of us sharing a bedroom. You would have left stuff behind. Clothes on the backs of chairs. Shaving foam. Bedroom slippers. Aftershave…'

His eyebrows shot up, his expression halting her in mid-flow.

'I have never spent a night in any woman's house and, if I had, I certainly wouldn't have left anything behind.'

Rosie's mouth fell open and she gaped at him. 'You've *never* stayed at a woman's overnight?' He was so arrogant, so beautiful, so sophisticated—she found it impossible to credit that he had never spent the night with a woman.

What woman, she guiltily thought, would let him out of her bed? It was an inappropriate thought but it lodged in her head, pounding with the steady force of a drum beat.

Matteo made a dismissive gesture with his hand that was both elegant and strangely exotic and she watched him from under lowered lashes, fascinated and mesmerised by the strong, proud lines of his handsome face.

'I'm a normal, red-blooded man with a healthy libido,' Matteo told her wryly. 'I work hard and I play hard, but I don't do love, and I never encourage a woman to think, even for a second, that I might.'

'And if you spent a night with a woman… it would mean that you're interested in more than just *sex*?'

'Forget about me,' Matteo drawled. 'The danger would lie in *her* believing that there might be more to it than sex.'

'And yet you're okay with spending time in the chalet with me?'

'Oh, but you're not my woman,' Matteo purred silkily. 'And this isn't about sex. This is a little pretend game that'll be over just as soon as I get what I'm after…'

CHAPTER THREE

ROSIE THOUGHT THAT it was one thing to produce Matteo as a boyfriend, like a magician pulling a rabbit from a hat then yanking him off stage before anyone had time to suss that it was all sleight of hand. It was something else to hold him up to scrutiny, which was what she would be doing by having him in the chalet with her. He would be spun around for inspection, asked questions, quizzed about his intentions. How was she going to deal with all that without cracking? How was *he*?

Her sisters, in particular, had all made it their mission to make Rosie keep them posted on her love life and she had always obliged. They had met a couple of her fleeting boyfriends and had not held back from making their opinions known, politely but firmly. She was so much younger than them and they had never really stopped treating her like the baby of the family.

Hence, Rosie thought with uncharacteristic bitterness, the reason why she was where she was now.

She had bolted from the prospect of having their idea of a suitable partner presented to her instead of standing her ground—but why on earth had it occurred to them that they could actually match her up with someone of their choosing in the first place?

This time, she was going to deal with the situation calmly. If there were too many questions, she would just stop answering. If the quizzing from Candice and Emily went too far, she would tell them to back off.

Matteo was a perfect stranger, but some of his remarks had been a little too perceptive for comfort. They had made her see herself in a different and more critical light than she had ever done before.

She wasn't silly and she didn't feel entitled but she *was* a trust-fund baby in the truest sense of the word and she had felt embarrassed to acknowledge the fact.

'You're going to be held up to the spotlight,' she warned. 'Five minutes with Candice is quite different to several days with my entire family.'

'I can take the heat,' Matteo drawled. 'Can you?'

Rosie looked at him steadily. 'I know what

you think of me,' she said, matching him for self-composure and liking the way she felt empowered by it. 'That I live off my parents, and float from one thing to the next and allow my entire family to have a say in my life, but this time round I am definitely going to take the heat.' She grinned suddenly. 'They'll be shocked.'

'Good,' Matteo murmured approvingly. 'Sometimes it's worthwhile to shock.'

'I just have one condition.'

'I'm all ears,' Matteo said wryly.

'I'm the one to do the breaking up.'

Matteo looked at her, at a loss for a suitable response.

'I can tell from your stunned expression that no one's ever broken up with you before, am I right? None of those women you refuse to spend the night with, just in case they get ideas, has ever broken up with you...?'

'Fate has smiled on me in that respect.'

'Well,' Rosie countered drily, 'Either smiled on you or else made you incredibly arrogant.'

Matteo grinned and then he burst out laughing. 'You're the most unexpected woman I've ever met,' he murmured. His eyes were lazy and shuttered and feathered over her like a caress. 'I've never met anyone as honest and outspoken. You contradict your background. So...

you want to break up with me. I don't see why not. Maybe it's high time I suffered from a broken heart, and it works for you, doesn't it?'

Rosie nodded slowly. 'I'm tired of my family feeling ever so slightly sorry for me.'

'So you dump the eligible guy and you instantly gain their respect. Well, we'll have to make sure that I'm the very besotted boyfriend, won't we? Now, why don't I check out of my suite here and we can both go to your chalet and begin this game…?'

His suite was breath-taking. Huge, with several rooms, including an open-plan kitchen, fully equipped but, she imagined, seldom used.

'You want this to be a convincing act?' he had put to her as they had emerged from the private room where they had been ensconced for ages. 'You come with me to my suite while I pack my things. Then we check out together. I was here on business when we met. Now that your family are coming over, it's only natural I shift base so that we can be together and meet them as a couple.'

Rosie looked at him as he efficiently gathered his belongings. While he packed, he conducted a series of calls in Italian, phone to his ear as he wandered from bedroom to living area, from bathroom to office, picking things up and tossing them in a case he had dumped on the glass table in the living area.

She got the feeling that he had forgotten about her completely.

'I don't know anything about you,' was the first thing she said when he was finally off the phone and the last of his things had been flung into the suitcase.

Here, in his suite, nerves assailed her. There was something so sleek and so innately *dangerous* about him that she found it impossible to think that they could convince her very perceptive and inquisitive family that they were really an item. Up close and personal, the force of his personality was more powerful, not less. She'd told herself that she wasn't going to be browbeaten by their curiosity and their questions, but how on earth were they going to believe that she, Rosie, bubbly, extrovert and carefree, had lost her heart to someone like Matteo?

Add to that the fact that he really was a stranger and the uphill task of convincing *anyone* seemed insurmountable.

In the act of zipping his suitcase, Matteo paused and looked at her for a few seconds.

She hadn't moved from her position by the door. She looked nervous and he marvelled that a lifetime of privilege—which had clearly been her background, judging from what she had told him—had managed to leave her unscathed. He hadn't been kidding when he had told her that she was unexpected. He met a lot of privileged people. Young and old, and even the most charming—they all had a very similar veneer of confidence borne from the assumption that the world was theirs for the asking. They all spoke loudly and with booming confidence. Most drew distinct lines between the people who served them and the people on their own level.

Rosie was as skittish as a kitten, open, guileless and honest to a fault, and that surprised and charmed him.

Now, looking at her, Matteo wondered whether he hadn't agreed to this charade because a part of him found her intriguing.

Rosie took a few hesitant steps forward and peered at the half-shut suitcase.

'You haven't brought any ski wear? Or have you stored it somewhere else?'

Matteo strolled to the small kitchen and withdrew a bottle of water from the fridge, which he held out to her. When she declined, he unscrewed the cap and drank.

'I don't ski,' he admitted. He dumped the empty bottle on the counter and hesitated momentarily, then he moved to the sofa and sat down, watching as she followed suit to sit facing him. 'And stop looking so nervous. I'm not going to pounce on you.'

'I know you're not.' She stifled a wave of nerves brought on by him telling her to stop looking nervous. 'We're not in public now. You know a lot about me, but I don't know anything about you, and I'm going to have to if our story is going to be credible. I'm surprised you don't ski,' she admitted.

'There's a time for learning to ski,' Matteo said wryly. 'It's fair to say I missed the slot.'

'Those obligatory school trips to the slopes can be a bore,' Rosie reminisced. 'I guess I'm lucky my parents were crazy about skiing. I can remember staring down fields of snow with little skis on when I was about three.' She laughed, throwing her head back, catching some of her hair in her hand and twisting it into a pony tail before releasing it.

Matteo smiled. 'Tell me more about your family. Your sister is married with two children and was a lawyer before she settled on motherhood...'

Rosie was transfixed by that smile. It was so genuinely curious that she felt her nerves begin to abate. She told him about Emily, sister number two and a chartered surveyor.

Also married. Pregnant with her first. She chatted about her parents. Her mother had been a lecturer and her father a high-ranking diplomat before they'd retired three years ago.

'And they didn't approve of past boy-friends,' he encouraged. 'Hence Bertie…'

Rosie grimaced. 'Hence Bertie. Not at all my type.'

'No? And what is your type, Rosie?'

Rosie opened her mouth to recite what she had always taken for granted—that she, free-spirited unlike her sisters, was attracted to other free spirited souls, unlike her brothers-in-law. Except, was she really?

He saved her from having to stumble through an answer by saying gently, 'You're very lucky. Riding lessons…skiing holidays from the age of three…house in the country and *pied à terre* in London. I'm guessing you dated guys your family didn't approve of as a form of quiet rebellion.'

'That's not true,' she countered but she could feel his observations too close to the bone. 'I've always been adventurous,' she concluded unconvincingly.

Matteo shrugged, ready to let it go and sur-prised that he had been lured into psycho-analysing her when he rarely felt inclined to plumb the depths of any woman.

'You wanted to know about me,' he said indifferently. 'Think of an upbringing as far from yours as it is possible to be.'

Rosie frowned. When she looked around her, all she could see was the trappings of wealth. He was clearly far, far richer than her parents or indeed anyone that she had ever known. He was in a league of his own and she didn't understand where he was going with that enigmatic remark.

He was sophisticated, polished and, if there was something of the street fighter about him, then she presumed that the richer you were the more ruthless you had to be.

'Did you grow up here? In Italy? I heard you on the phone, speaking in Italian...'

'I was born here but my parents went to England in search of a better life when I was a baby.' Matteo paused, uncomfortable with sharing details of his past but knowing that she was entitled to information up to a point. 'There was nothing for them here in Italy and they were young and hopeful. Unfortunately, life did not quite work out the way they planned. My mother contracted a virus shortly after they arrived in England, and was taken into hospital, but by the time they diagnosed meningitis it was too late.'

Rosie covered her mouth with her hand and

stared at him. There was a remoteness about his features that mirrored the cool briskness of his voice. He was stating facts with all emotion removed from the recital. More than anything, she felt her heart twist at that. It was a defence mechanism to protect himself from the pain of losing a parent at such a young age. That was something she felt instinctively, just as she also knew instinctively that this proud, arrogant man would not appreciate her sharing her thoughts with him.

In that moment, he was so very human that she wanted to reach out and touch him. She sat on her hands just in case they decided to disobey the warning bells in her head telling her to avoid any such spontaneous show of affection.

'I'm so sorry, Matteo,' she contented herself by saying and he lowered his eyes, thick lashes brushing his aristocratic cheekbones, before he looked at her once again, fully composed.

'Don't be. It's history.'

'And where is your father now?' she asked. 'Does he live over here? He must have been devastated at the time. Did he return to Italy?'

'My father died when I was four and I was taken into foster care. No, he did not return to Italy. I have maintained my links, however. I have a villa on the outskirts of Venice and at the moment I'm in the process of expanding my operations to Naples. Hence my conference call earlier.'

'Foster care?'

'It's of no importance.' He stood up and glanced around, making sure that he was leaving nothing behind.

Rosie thought differently. It was of monumental importance and it gave her valuable insight into this forbidding stranger now phoning down for a porter to come and collect his belongings.

He was so cold, she thought, so contained, and there was a very good reason for that.

He was walking towards the door and she shot to her feet and hurried behind him. Instead of opening the door, however, he stared down at her, his dark eyes shuttered.

'The only reason I've told you what I have,' he stated, 'Is because you have a point. Relationships aren't built on two people knowing absolutely nothing about one another, and this has to be a credible relationship until all the paperwork is done on the deal I'm working on with Bob and Margaret.'

'You haven't told me why it's so important.'

'Nor will I. And I should tell you that you should save the questions if any of them involve further delving into my past. I've given you sufficient information for us to pull this charade off. The confidences end there. The fact is we are not in a relationship. This is a temporary and fictitious arrangement and all we need to establish is a sufficiently credible basis from which we can answer the most straightforward questions.' He opened the door and they walked in silence to the lift, then rode down to the busy foyer.

All the while, thoughts were buzzing around in her head like wasps. He had opened a door and, having peered in, she wanted to have another look.

As soon as they were back in the public domain, he slung his arm over her shoulders, only breaking apart to sign himself out.

There was a background hum of Christmas carols being played which followed them out of the hotel onto the snow-covered slopes.

Rosie had been to many ski resorts with her family over the years but they had fallen in love with this one and had made it their annual destination. The ski resort was situated in the heart of the Southern Alps in the Veneto region of Northern Italy. From here, Venice was a couple of hours away, and she figured that Matteo had probably arranged for his clients to come to this particular resort because it had suited him. He couldn't have picked a more beautiful spot for the un-initiated.

The mountainous, pink and orange back-drop of the Dolomites was picture-postcard perfect, soaring up, commanding the valley and everything nestled inside it. The vista never failed to impress and Rosie stopped and stared at the sight.

'You don't know what you're missing.' She turned to him impulsively.

'Meaning?'

'You should learn to ski. I could teach you.' She laughed at the horror etched on Matteo's lean face and slowly he grinned.

'You don't give up, do you?' he murmured, staring out at the panoramic view with her. Out here, everything was shrouded in silence, and the hue from the rising mountains was quite special. He had always used his Venetian villa as a bolthole. It had never occurred to him that this glorious place existed. But then again, he didn't ski, so why would it have?

He gazed back down to her upturned face. She had dimples when she smiled. She had stuffed a woolly hat on her head and her tan-gled white-blonde curls trailed in disarray from under it. Wrapped up in countless lay-ers, her small, curvaceous body was tempting beyond endurance and Matteo spun around on his heels, indicating that they should make for her car now.

'What do you mean?' Rosie tripped alongside him, keeping some distance but feeling the impact of his presence slamming into her at every step.

'I mean, others would have tactfully retreated once I warned them off trying to get to know me.'

'That's very egotistical of you.' She swerved into the hotel car park, heading towards the four-wheel-drive car that was kept on permanent standby, as the villa was used by the family out of season as well.

'Egotistical?'

'I don't want to get to know you,' Rosie lied, beeping open the doors and hoisting herself into the driver's seat. She waited until he was sitting in the passenger seat before turning to him. In the late-evening light he was all shadows and angles, and he sent a shiver of fierce excitement racing down her spine. 'I just thought that, if we're going to be stuck with one another for days on end, it might give us something to do aside from arguing, and anyway, it's a shame to be here and not try your hand at it.'

She started the engine and the car shuddered into life.

'I've never had any woman tell me that she has to think of things to do if she's going to be stuck with me,' Matteo said, amused in spite of himself. 'Sure you know how to handle this thing in snowy terrain?'

'The road to the chalet is clear and gritted, Matteo, so there's no need to be nervous—and of course I know how to handle it.' She glanced across at him. 'Don't tell me that you think women can't drive as good as men?'

'Can they, though?'

Rosie heard the lazy teasing in his voice and she burst out laughing.

Her heart skipped a beat. A thread of something beyond excitement suddenly sparked and sizzled in her veins.

'Probably better.' She was focused one hundred percent on the road ahead of her, taking it very slowly, but she didn't want to lose the moment. She liked this. 'Are you scared of giving it a go? The skiing, I mean?'

'Terrified,' Matteo drawled.

'I'll make sure you're all right.'

'Will you, now? That's an offer that's almost too good to pass up.'

They were nearing the chalet—a left-hand turn off the main road and then just a short drive to the warmth of the ski lodge. The drive was short but hazardous, but the car was equipped for all conditions and handled the steep climb to the chalet with aplomb. Ahead, the bright lights were welcoming.

Candice was waiting for them, dressed to go out but making sure she stayed put to ask questions. Having shaken off the snow, hung various jackets and coats and dumped shoes and boots and all the other paraphernalia, Rosie faced her elegant, glamorous sister with a strength of purpose she had never really experienced before.

From behind, she was aware of Matteo approaching, but the touch of his hand on her waist, curving to rest just under her breasts, still made her flush. She hesitantly slipped her arm around him to complete the picture she knew he was striving to convey. The pressure of his palm on her rib cage and the crazy tingling of her nipples in heated response fogged up her brain and she knew that she was beetroot-red.

She wanted to moan and chewed down on her lip in horror, especially when he lazily circled his fingers on the woolly jumper, applying just the right amount of pressure.

She had whipped off the woolly hat and in a matter of a few heart-stopping seconds he sifted his fingers into her hair and tilted her chin so that she was gazing up at him. Then he lowered his mouth to graze over hers…and all those things she had read about in magazines suddenly made complete sense. Lust…desire…whatever you wanted to call it…

She had had one serious relationship that had, in retrospect, been nothing more than the optimism of youth to be loved and a need to be rescued from her abortive university career. It had lasted a matter of months and had certainly not prepared her for the high-voltage charge of craving that shot through her body when his lips met hers. Nothing she had ever experienced had. Confusion tore into her, darkening her eyes, sending a slight tremble through her body.

Her vocal cords seemed to have dried up, but it didn't matter, because Candice was smiling and Matteo had eased into charismatic gear and was saying all the right things, asking all the right questions, giving her cool, contained sister little chance of asking questions back.

'I'd really love to hear about the two of you and how you met.' She glanced at her watch, while from the sidelines Rosie breathed a sigh of relief. 'But I'm going to catch up with some friends I haven't seen for ages. Before the family descend tomorrow evening. By the way, they can't wait to meet you. Hope you don't mind but I couldn't help but share the news with everyone—and get them to hold off on trying to set you up with Bertie.'

'Actually,' Rosie heard herself say, 'I do mind, Diss. It was my place to tell them that Matteo and I are…er…going out.'

'Yes, I suppose so but…' Bright colour poured into Candice's cheeks. For the first time in living memory, she was discomfited by her much younger sister, and Rosie realised that this was what she should have been doing all along. Taking control of her life and owning her decisions.

'It's done now,' she said quietly. 'It doesn't matter.' Oddly, Matteo's hand cupping the nape of her neck gave her a certain amount of strength.

'I do apologise, Rosie. I was just so excited that you'd actually met someone…'

Candice shifted, aware that she was treading in unchartered waters, accustomed as she was to compliance from her younger sister.

'Socially acceptable?' Matteo interjected coolly. He tightened his hold on Rosie and she leant against him, loving the strength he imparted. He was as solid as a rock.

'That's not quite what I meant.' Candice reddened.

'My track record hasn't been great,' Rosie said appeasingly.

Candice gave her a bright, relieved smile and moved towards her for a quick hug before standing back and looking at them both with her head to one side.

'You two make a fantastic couple,' she said. 'I was quite prepared to thump you when Rosie told me that you'd let her down. I can't tell you how happy I am for the both of you that whatever misunderstanding you had has been sorted. I can just tell that you're meant for one another.' She winked at her sister.

'Hang on, Candice,' Rosie interjected, horrified and embarrassed that 'holiday fling' was morphing into 'marriage on the cards'. 'We've really only just met! We're still getting to know one another.'

Candice was laughing, heading for the door. 'That's how all relationships begin, Rosie! Anyway, don't wait up for me, guys. That car could pull a sled in an avalanche, but if I feel too tired to head back then I'll just stay over with Mick and Carol. They've already invited me and they've got oodles of room. I'll text and let you know.'

With which she left in a flurry of air kisses,

slamming the door behind her, leaving Rosie alone with Matteo.

'So...' He looked around him. 'Nice place, Rosie.' It was open-plan, big but not huge, and with all the clutter of hectic family life left behind from one holiday to the other— well-thumbed books, games, toys and all sorts of bits and pieces collected over the years. The floors were deep, rich wood and there was a clutter of artwork on the walls, pictures done by Rosie and her sisters. In the sitting area, colourful throws were tossed onto the deep, comfortable sofas, and in the corner the television was rumbling on, volume low, because Candice had forgotten to switch it off.

Looking around her, Rosie saw the place through his eyes. It was the essence of upper-middle-class comfort.

'Can I ask you something?' She waited until he had turned full circle to look at her.

'Ask away.'

'I know you said you didn't want me prying into your private life...'

Matteo realised that her prying was a lot less objectionable than expected. He wondered whether that was because, for the first time in his life, he had opened up about his past with another human being. Of course, he had had very little choice, given the situation, and none of it mattered anyway, because they would be parting company before Santa dropped down the chimney with his sack of goodies, but it was still a little unnerving.

He wasn't the confiding sort and he grimly told himself that he wasn't going to change any time soon. A leopard never changed its spots and his reticence was solidly ingrained. He had always lived his life with the assumption that, when it came to other people and his private life, information was purely on a need-to-know basis.

Like now, was what sprang to mind.

'Then don't,' he informed her silkily.

'I was just curious to find out how you... ended up where you did.'

'Rich and powerful?' He sat on one of the squashy sofas, which was a lot more comfortable than the pale leather ones in his place in London. He thought of that halfway house and the boisterous fun he had had there all those years ago. He'd never thought he would ever laugh again after he'd been put into foster care, but he had. The place had been designed to broaden the horizons of the underprivileged kids who went there and it had worked, at least for him.

'There's that modesty of yours again,'

Rosie teased lightly, but her curiosity was getting the better of her fast and she joined him on the sofa, opposite end, but close enough to hear every word he was saying.

'When you're a kid in care, you have to make an effort not to slide down to the lowest common denominator,' Matteo told her conversationally. 'No one has any dreams for you. You have to make sure you have dreams for yourself or you sink to the bottom fast. I was lucky. I was bright. I learned the value of education.' He shrugged. 'I studied. I never skipped class. I set my sights on the only thing that mattered.'

'What was that?'

'Freedom. When you grow up without any advantages, money is the only thing that buys freedom, and by the age of eighteen I'd come to the conclusion that I would just have to make money and a lot of it. I was gifted at maths and got into Cambridge University. Got a first-class degree and was lucky enough to get taken on by a burgeoning investment bank. By twenty-five I'd made my first million. The bonuses were insane, but that life didn't suit me. I don't like taking orders or working for other people. So I jacked it in and began scouting around for companies to buy.

Small IT companies, mainly. That's the long and short of it. Rags to riches.'

'Your opinion of me must be very low.' She thought of her cosseted background, the trust fund that kept her going, the university career she had jettisoned because she had been bored stiff.

Matteo looked at her. She had such a transparent face. Yes, he really should have a low opinion of her, but there was something about her...

'You're not the sort of woman I would normally be drawn to,' he was forced to concede.

She raised aquamarine eyes to his, and his jaw tightened, because she was hurt.

'That's not meant to be an insult, Rosie,' he said roughly.

'I know that. It's the truth. What sort of women *are* you drawn to, just out of interest?'

'Career women,' he admitted.

'Of course.'

'We're poles apart,' he reminded her. 'I'm sure you wouldn't, under normal circumstances, go for someone like me.'

'Definitely not.' Rosie tilted her chin at a mutinous angle, pride coming to her rescue, because it cut to the quick that, whether he found her sexy or not—and she hated herself for dwelling on that stupid, throwaway compliment—he would never have given her the time of day if he hadn't been dumped into playing out this charade. 'I'm just shocked at how easily Candice fell for the charade,' she mused truthfully.

'People believe what they want to believe,' Matteo said with a shrug. 'Human nature. Your family want what they think is best for you and someone rich, powerful and wearing a suit fits the narrative.' He looked at her. 'And here's another reason why no one will question this too deeply…'

Matteo looked at her flushed, pretty face ,but then his eyes drifted down to the tightness of her jumper straining over full breasts and the curve of her hips.

The atmosphere shifted. He could feel it and he knew that she would as well. He was just looking, he thought, because he wasn't going to encourage any further complication to an already complicated and annoying situation. He was going to be sticking around for a handful of days and then he would be off, leaving her to assert her independence and damn him for the bastard he really wasn't at all.

'What's that?' Rosie asked breathlessly.

'The most obvious reason of all. Opposites attract…'

CHAPTER FOUR

ROSIE COULD ONLY concede the truth behind that statement. Matteo was sinfully good-looking but he wasn't her type. Take away the dark good looks and the perfectly honed, intensely masculine physique, and what you had was your basic businessman, the sort of guy to appeal to her entire family but not to her.

It was true that she had never met any businessman quite in this one's league but he was still nothing like the free-spirited adventurers towards whom she always gravitated. She shouldn't be attracted to him at all but she was.

But then, he wasn't exactly Mr Typical Business Tycoon, was he?

That background in foster care…

Not exactly your run-of-the mill CEO…

And those cool, cool eyes…seeing everything and revealing nothing…also not typical.

And that thread-like scar…where had that come from? Surely not filling out profit and loss columns with his fountain pen?

'She took it for granted, your sister,' Matteo said conversationally. 'That it was okay to break the news about us in a group family chat without asking whether you might have preferred to do the news-breaking yourself. That par for the course? Because, if it is, then you did well to put her in her place.' He settled his gaze on her.

'I know,' Rosie said simply. She didn't add that his presence had given her backbone. 'The problem is that Candice wouldn't have relayed the information the way I would have.'

'Explain.'

'You heard her. She thinks this is some great romance and that's what she would have told everyone. I would have been a little more realistic. I would have prepared them for the fact that there was a chance this wasn't going to work out. It feels as though things are getting more and more difficult to control.'

'That's the problem when a lie begins to spiral out of control.'

She was hovering.

Things had taken an unexpected turn and he could see that she was uncomfortable with the situation. Her edginess was apparent in the way her gaze was flicking towards him, then flicking away…in the way her whole body seemed alive with restlessness even though she wasn't actually moving around. Underneath the feisty, open exterior, real apprehension was creeping in. The consequences of that little white lie were dawning on her.

'It's also the problem with acting on impulse but, if you think you've been inconvenienced, then I should tell you that the last thing I'd banked on doing was remaining here for longer than strictly necessary.'

'I'm sure you have commitments. It's Christmas.'

'I don't do Christmas. The only reason I'm here at this time of year was because of the timing on this deal. My only commitment was to retreat to my villa outside Venice and escape the madness.'

'Escape? *Escape?*' Distracted, she angled her bright, blue-eyed gaze in his direction.

'Don't look so bewildered.' Matteo's eyebrows winged up. 'Not everyone is in love with the festive season.'

'You have no family…' Rosie said slowly.

'Don't go there,' Matteo told her, voice dropping by several degrees.

Rosie frowned. 'It must be a lonely time of year for you,' she said simply and Matteo vaulted to his feet and frustratedly raked hands through his hair.

'What is it about *stay out of my private life* that you don't get?'

Rosie didn't apologise. Her mind was busy with images of him in foster care. He had given her a sketchy description of what it had been like but she knew that it probably would have been far more soul-destroying. He had expressly set up No Trespass signs and he had made it clear that the only reason he had said anything at all was because he'd felt it necessary.

Except...her heart went out to him. She knew that she was going where no doubt angels feared to tread, but there was a generosity of spirit inside her that found it difficult to leave the subject alone.

'Everyone needs to talk to somebody about the distressing things that happen in their lives.'

'I don't believe I'm hearing this! I don't think you quite understood...'

'You don't want to talk about it.' She shrugged but her clear blue eyes were stubbornly fixed on his face as he towered over her, looking down, expression forbidding.

'No,' Matteo said with angry force. 'I don't.'

'Which says a lot.'

Matteo leant over her, hands on either side of her, depressing the soft sofa cushions and caging her in. His face was dark with enraged incredulity that someone had dared cross the boundary lines he had laid down. Did the woman have *no* limits when it came to saying what was on her mind? Matteo was accustomed to people editing their behaviour around him. Her lack of interest in following those rules left him practically speechless. From the second she had appeared in his life, normal rules of behaviour had been suspended.

'Don't make me regret having told you what I did.'

'Why would you regret it?'

'Are you hearing a word I'm saying?'

She held his outraged stare. 'You're accustomed to everyone doing what you tell them to do, aren't you?'

Matteo stood up but remained standing in front of her.

'Yes, I am!'

'Okay. You win! I won't ask and you don't have to tell me anything. Would you like something to eat? Drink?' She stood up and swerved around him, heading to the kitchen and straight to the fridge to peer inside.

As always it was crammed with food. A lot of optimistically healthy options that were probably past their sell-by date. She had been staying at the chalet since the season had begun and she was an impulse shopper. Things in attractive jars always held so much promise but often it was the easiest way she ended up taking.

He was still scowling when she looked at him quizzically. 'Well?' she snapped. 'You don't want to talk to me about anything of any importance, so we can talk about food options instead. I know you'll think it's safer. What do you want? I can make you something.'

Matteo wasn't into women cooking for him. In fact, he actively discouraged it, just as he always made sure that a night of pleasure never turned into breakfast together the following morning.

'I usually just eat stuff that comes out of boxes or cans but I don't suppose you do.'

'I don't,' Matteo said flatly. He paused. 'You ask a lot of questions.'

'So do you.' Her azure eyes were innocent and her voice was sincere because she meant it.

'Show me the rest of your house.'

Rosie shook herself back to earth, hesitating and on the cusp of barrelling past his Keep Out sign but reluctantly accepting that, if he wasn't into sharing, then he wasn't into sharing. They meant nothing to one another and she would have to put her curiosity to bed because it wasn't going to get her anywhere.

She gave a perfunctory tour: open-plan living area with a huge, modern fireplace and lots of comfy chairs, perfect for settling in for the long haul—just her, a book and the fall of silent snow outside. The kitchen, which was the hub of the house, and a study in which her father occasionally worked, although now that he had retired those instances were few and far between. He had forgone offers of consultancy jobs and opted for quality time with his family instead.

Wooden stairs led to the floor above: six bedrooms all leading onto a broad landing that overlooked the space below. Next to her, Matteo's silence was oppressive, and she wondered what was going through his head.

She found out soon enough.

'So where is our bedroom?'

About to head back downstairs, head still buzzing with unanswered questions, Rosie spun around on her heels and stared at him with consternation.

'You can choose which bedroom you'd like,' she told him politely. 'Mine...' she nodded in the direction of the bedroom at the end of the long, broad landing '...is down there.'

'Well, I suppose that's where I'll be dumping my bags.'

He headed down at pace towards her bedroom and, as he flung open the door, she was right behind him.

She'd waved an arm to indicate the bedroom floor, only opening the first door and standing back while he'd looked inside like a prospective buyer doing a tour of a house. Now, with him standing in her bedroom, her personal space, she felt invaded. She was on show here, with all the little pieces of her childhood for him to see. A framed photo of her on her first horse, with her dad proudly standing next to her. The ridiculous chair in the shape of a big, pink heart which had been her favourite when she'd been about eight, and which her parents had stashed away in their attic, shipping it over when they'd bought the chalet years before. Pictures of her family over the years.

'You're not staying in *my* bedroom,' She

folded her arms and watched, tight-lipped, as he strolled through the bedroom, peering at this and that and ignoring her. He had dumped his bag on the ground like a declaration of intent that sent a chill of forbidden excitement racing up and down her spine.

He commanded the space around him. He was so tall...so muscular...so *there*.

'Oh.' He spun round and stared right back at her. 'This is exactly where I'll be staying.' As if to confirm what he'd said, he picked up the designer bag and flung it on the mattress of her four-poster bed.

It landed with a soft *thud* and then sat there, challenging her to remove it.

'But...'

'No *buts*. You got me into this mess and, now I'm in it, for better or for worse you're just going to have to suffer the consequences. We're supposed to be an item. Hot off the press, so to speak. Your sister is going to be extremely suspicious if she thinks that we're not sharing a bedroom. Particularly given the fact that she probably assumes that you've been sharing my suite at the hotel while we've been conducting our torrid affair.' He glanced at his watch then back to her, where she had remained hovering at the doorway to her own bedroom, almost as though, having asserted his authority, *she* was now the guest in her own space.

'I can tell her that we're in separate rooms here out of respect for Mum and Dad.'

'That's ridiculous.'

'You don't know my parents!'

'Are you telling me that you would be exiled to the Arctic wastes if they discovered that we were sleeping together?' He pinned his eyes to her reddening face. 'Right. Enough said on the subject.'

Rosie's face was a picture of dawning dismay. Their love-at-first-sight scenario invited enough questions without those questions reaching fever pitch because they were in separate bedrooms, like a Victorian couple.

'Now,' Matteo declared, jettisoning the subject as if suddenly bored with the whole thing, 'I would come down and have something out of a box or a can with you, but right now I want a shower, and I have a stack of emails to get through, so I'll have to forfeit the feast.'

He reached for the button on his trousers and Rosie stared open-mouthed for a few seconds before gathering her wits.

'I hadn't banked on this,' she said tightly and he stared at her with disbelieving eyes.

'And I hadn't banked on it either,' he informed her coolly. 'Right about now, I should have been getting in touch with my housekeeper and readying her for my arrival. Instead…'

Instead, she mentally filled in, *here you are, sharing a room with a woman you don't know, who keeps getting on your nerves with her constant questions, caught up in a crazy game of make-believe.*

'If you're sure you're not hungry…' she muttered, inching a couple of steps back, eyes still fixed on him. She didn't want to, but she couldn't help feverishly wondering what he looked like underneath the expensive clothes. Bronzed and sinewy, she imagined, every cord and muscle defined. She felt faint thinking about it and, when she contemplated the prospect of sharing her bedroom with him, she went into a positive mental tailspin. She eyed the *chaise longue* by the window.

'You can make that up.' She nodded in the direction of the *chaise longue*. 'It's very comfortable.'

Matteo didn't say anything. He glanced at it, his hooded silver eyes revealing nothing. 'Like I said,' he drawled, 'I'll do without the food. Now, unless you have no objection to seeing me strip off in front of you…?'

Colour high in her cheeks, Rosie fled, shutting the door behind her.

In the quiet of the kitchen, she hastily prepared some pasta for herself, making good use of a number of tins. Comfort eating. Her head was full of the ramifications of her very small, practically invisible little white lie. Everything had snowballed and now here she was, with the sexiest man on the planet upstairs in her bedroom. Her nerves were shredded. When she thought of Matteo, everything inside her went into meltdown. Physically, she felt faint when she closed her eyes and pictured him in all his over-the-top sexiness. He was just so breathtakingly *beautiful*.

But it wasn't just confined to the way he looked. If that had been the sum total of it, then she could have steeled herself against the impact, because a good-looking guy without personality was just a cardboard cut-out to be admired without any threat of him getting under your skin.

No. Matteo's extraordinary effect on her was all wrapped up in the power of his personality, his air of command, and now that she had eked out a couple of personal details the fallibility she could sense underneath the cloak of arrogant self-assurance.

He posed questions, he ignited her imagination, he stirred depths of curiosity she'd never known she possessed.

Absorbed in hectic speculation, she ate without thinking—the pasta, some salad that looked dangerously close to needing last rites performed then a slab of chocolate dessert that was just the thing to settle her mind.

She was startled when she heard the sound of the door opening and then there was Candice, shedding outer layers of snow-covered gear as she breezed into the kitchen, pink-faced and smiling.

'I really miss the little monsters.' She headed straight to the fridge to pull out a bottle of mineral water. 'But—' she looked at Rosie with a grin '—some time out is a wonderful thing. Had a ball. So nice to catch up with that crew. Where's Matteo?'

'He's...um...working.'

'Working?' She kept her eyes fixed on Rosie's flushed face as she drank from the bottle before lowering it. 'Where? In Dad's office? Surely he can pack in the work for a few days...if he's head over heels in love with you?'

'Well, you know how it goes when it comes to men and...er...work.' Rosie offered vaguely. Her sisters had always had the ability to pin her to the spot with their penetrating blue eyes and she was pinned to the spot now, unable to move forward and incapable of shuffling back.

'Tell me.'

'Lucien works all the hours under the sun, or have you forgotten?'

'He's a surgeon,' Candice responded drily. 'Lives depend on him. It's early days for you both, Rosie. I would have expected him to have made a little time for you, especially considering the time of year, when most businesses are operating at a much slower pace.'

Rosie remained steadfastly silent. A fierce defensiveness for her so-called boyfriend suddenly kicked into gear allied to the stubborn need to stand her ground. Where had that come from?

'He isn't where he is because he's a slacker, Candice,' she said without the usual note of apology in her voice. 'Sometimes work can take over, and not necessarily because lives are at stake. Lucien might save lives on an operating table, but Matteo and how he runs his businesses can affect the livelihoods of lots of people who work for him.'

Candice stared.

'I consider myself duly told off. Second time for the evening. The only reason I sound nosy...' She sighed. 'Okay, I've researched the guy,' she confessed, 'And he's big stuff, Rosie. Somewhere at the back of my mind, I recognised the name, but I honestly thought I was mistaken because I couldn't believe that someone who doesn't even breathe the same air as we do could...well...'

'Find me attractive? Thanks very much.'

'It's not that at all!' Candice said quickly. 'I can't help being protective of you—he's out of your league, Rosebud. For a start, the sort of women he dates...'

'I know. He likes high-powered career women.'

'So he told you? I'm impressed with his honesty on that front, at least. Of course, Emily's heard of him, and so has Robert. But, from everything I've read and heard, he's so far up the pecking order that you literally have to be a billionaire to have much personal contact with him at all on the business level.'

Frankly, Rosie couldn't help thinking, the more Candice elaborated, the less likely it seemed that someone like Matteo would even glance in the direction of someone like her. Not unless they had temporarily taken leave of their senses. Christmas madness. Except, he didn't do Christmas.

'But of course,' Candice continued, flipping open the bin and dumping the plastic bottle into the recycling section, 'Opposites *do* attract, I'll give you that.'

'They do…' Rosie smiled to herself, remembering what Matteo had said earlier.

'There's no accounting for people when they fall in love.'

Fall in love? Was that the story doing the rounds? And was it spreading like a forest fire beyond the family unit?

'Well…' She laughed lightly and managed to galvanise her body into action, walking across to sit opposite her sister, wishing she had opted for a restorative glass of wine, for some Dutch courage would have done wonders right now. 'I don't know about *falling in love…*'

'What do you mean?'

'Relationships aren't all about *falling in love*,' she asserted, glancing away.

'That's not what you've always maintained,' Candice told her drily. She paused and delivered a searching look to her sister. 'I don't want you to get hurt,' she said quietly. 'And I'm very much afraid that you will. I just don't think you're tough enough to handle a guy like Matteo.'

Into the brief silence came the last voice either of them expected to hear.

'Maybe that's what I find so charming about your sister.'

They both looked up to see that Matteo had silently pushed open the kitchen door and was now lounging in the doorframe.

How long had he been there?

Rosie tried to remember if she had said anything incriminating and was certain that she hadn't.

He'd showered and changed into a pair of faded jeans and an old tee shirt and he looked drop-dead gorgeous—easy, relaxed, wildly sophisticated and with that edge of danger about him that made her whole body go on full alert.

'Maybe,' Matteo continued, 'It's a breath of fresh air to be with a woman who isn't as tough as nails and doesn't want to spend every minute of her time discussing the state of the world and how it should be fixed.' He strolled towards Rosie and then remained standing behind her, his hands on her shoulders, lightly caressing her neck and feathering shivers of pleasure through her body.

He leant to brush his lips on the nape of her neck and she nearly passed out.

She had never seen Candice out of her depth but Matteo unsettled her, Rosie thought. It was his self-assurance, his bone-deep confidence that his opinions carried weight. He didn't *allow* anyone to take advantage of him and, before they thought that they could try, he made sure to establish the lines of command.

'And what makes you think that your sister will be the one to be hurt?' he enquired coolly.

'Exactly.' Rosie finally entered the conversation but her usual spirited response was seriously compromised by the continuing, caressing motion of his fingers on her neck. 'Candice, please don't worry about me.'

'I intend to take very good care of your sister.' Matteo's voice was still cool.

'Really?' Candice's eyebrows shot up. 'I mean, I hope so. We all do.'

'Why would I say it if I didn't mean it?'

'But,' Rosie interjected, 'It's only been a couple of weeks so...we're taking each day as it comes.'

'And you were always the impulsive one, Rosie,' Candice teased. 'Is love changing you already?'

'Don't be ridiculous!' Rosie spluttered. How much deeper could the hole she had dug for herself go?

'I know it's not wedding bells yet!' Candice laughed and stood up, her movements graceful as she strode towards the door. 'But please don't forget to give me ample warning so that I can start planning my outfit!'

Rosie managed to stammer out something, grateful that Matteo seemed to be taking it all in his stride, and it was only when the kitchen door was shut and her sister well and truly gone that Rosie looked at him with alarm.

'You should never have encouraged my sister to think that there was more to this than there is!' was the first thing she said, leaping to her feet, irritated at Matteo's composure as he helped himself to a bottle of water from the fridge.

'We should head up,' was all he said.

'Why on earth did you come down here, anyway? I thought you said that you had a mountain of emails to get through!'

'The prospect of working suddenly didn't seem quite so enticing.' He circled her and stared down at her for a few seconds until she reluctantly lifted her eyes to his.

'I was trying to ease the way to us breaking up,' she confessed. 'Until you came along and demolished all my efforts. Why couldn't you have just taken the lead from me and backed me up when I started insinuating that this was probably just a fling?'

Matteo shrugged. 'Maybe I'm so arrogant

that the thought of being written off as a fling dented my ego.'

'I don't believe you,' Rosie muttered.

'Maybe...' he murmured.

Rosie didn't know what was going through his head, but his expression wasn't the expression of an arrogant alpha male with a sore ego.

'Just maybe it got on my nerves hearing your sister assume that a man like me could never look twice at someone like you.'

'I'm not asking for your pity.'

'If you don't assert yourself, you'll be walked over.'

'Thank you very much for the words of advice.'

'You've stood up to your sister once. You can do it again. Try it a few times and you might find that it becomes a way of life.'

'You don't like me prying into your private life, Matteo, and I don't like you thinking that you can analyse me.'

'But you've set a precedent. Don't get me wrong,' he grated. 'Your life is none of my business but it affronts something in me when I hear you being treated like a kid who needs other people to look after her. You're not a kid.'

'I know that,' Rosie muttered grudgingly.

She sneaked a glance at him from under her lashes. 'I did actually stick up for you when she told me that it was strange for you to be working when you should be desperate to spend time in my company.'

'Did you, now?'

Rosie could see the speculation in his eyes at that admission. 'I thought it might be a good idea to let her know that work came first with you.'

Matteo burst out laughing, his grey eyes darkening with appreciation. 'More of those foundations being laid down.'

'It might have been if you had got on board with me instead of branching out and doing your own thing.'

Matteo shrugged, the smile lingering on his lips, and began heading towards the door. 'I'm hitting the sack. Coming?'

'I'll… I think I'll stay down here and finish tidying the kitchen,' Rosie told him. For a while she'd forgotten the prospect ahead of sharing her bedroom with him but it was all coming back to her now at great speed. On the spot she decided that she would stay out of harm's way in the kitchen, at least long enough for him to fall asleep so that when she finally joined him he would be dead to the world.

She couldn't picture him being dead to the world, though. In fact, she couldn't imagine him sleeping. More lying still with his eyes closed but primed to leap into action at the sound of a pin dropping.

'Don't wait up. There's linen in the cupboard on the landing for the *chaise longue*.'

'Sure.' He didn't bother turning around to look at her but left the kitchen, shutting the door behind him, leaving her to take as long as she possibly could filling the dishwasher, wiping the counters and in the end going through the contents of the fridge and binning everything that no longer had any lifespan left whatsoever.

It was after midnight by the time she finally headed up to the bedroom and she was dead on her feet.

So he was going to be in her bedroom. That meant nothing. She was going to be cool and composed because he was right—she wasn't a kid and she was going to stop behaving like one. She was the only one who could determine the direction of her life and her choices and she was going to remember that.

This felt like a crucial moment for her. She was at a crossroads. She either carried on in no particular direction, escaping her family's well-intentioned guidance by drifting from one job to another, or else she buckled down and asserted herself. It was odd that a perfect stranger had been the one to bring her to this point.

He told her things that she didn't want to hear but it was thanks to him that she had actually stood up to Candice instead of backing away. She had always been treated like the baby of the family and she had followed through, fulfilling their expectations, becoming the family member happy to drift through life while other people got on with responsible living and grown-up decision making.

When she stood back and looked at it through objective eyes, she was mortified.

From now on, things were going to change. They already had.

Filled with the rosy glow of assertiveness, Rosie pushed open the bedroom door and there he was on the *chaise longue*, semireclining, and it looked painful. His laptop was open and his legs looked as though they weren't quite sure where they should go. Over the end of the sofa? Uncomfortable. On the ground? Likewise. He was way too tall and too big for the piece of furniture to which he had been consigned but the fact that he had obeyed orders touched her.

He shifted his big, muscular bulk as she

walked in, drawing attention… Forget about the inadequacies of his makeshift bed, the guy was semi-naked.

Low-slung, loose-fitting jogging bottoms. That was it. He was half-naked and she stood by the door, shamelessly gaping for a few seconds, before walking in and shutting the door behind her.

Thank God he hadn't switched on the overhead light. Instead, he had swivelled the anglepoise lamp by the bed in the direction of the *chaise longue*. Rosie hoped that in a half-dark room the beetroot red of her cheeks wouldn't immediately be visible.

'You took your time,' Matteo said, now standing up and stretching before dumping the laptop on her dressing table.

Rosie's vocal cords had dried up. She cleared her throat and stared straight past his spectacular, burnished bronze body to the window just behind him. Seemed a safer option. That said, he still managed to intrude into the entire periphery of her vision. He was so tall, muscles densely packed, the flat lines of his stomach tapering to a narrow waist and spirals of dark hair arrowing down…

'There was a lot of tidying to do in the kitchen,' she croaked. 'You… I see you've made yourself comfortable on the *chaise longue*.'

Matteo glanced over his shoulder and grimaced. 'I'm not sure that *comfortable* would be the appropriate word.'

Rosie had expected complaints. Maybe a show of resentful acceptance of the boundaries she had laid down, possibly even fully fledged refusal to accommodate her wishes. But his voice was remarkably even and she felt something...quite different from those waves of taboo attraction. She felt the stirrings of affection.

She glanced at her lovely king-sized bed and Matteo followed the direction of her gaze.

'I'm in your house,' he said, walking to the window and back to the sofa, exercising his long limbs. 'The bed is yours.'

'I'm half your size.'

'Rules of the house apply here,' Matteo drawled drily, flexing his muscles again and then sinking back down onto the *chaise longue*, his dark eyes pinned to her face as she remained hovering like a visitor in her own bedroom. He grinned. 'Relax. There's no need to start thinking about playing the self-sacrificing martyr by giving up your bed for me, Rosie. If the shoe was on the other foot and you were in my house, I'd be sprawled out on the bed and you'd be trying to squeeze into the clothes hamper in the bathroom. It's late. Forget I'm here and go to sleep.'

CHAPTER FIVE

THE BEDROOM WAS empty the following morning when Rosie woke up. In that moment between sleeping and waking, she had a brief respite when she actually forgot about Matteo being in her room at all, then she shot up into a sitting position and squinted at the *chaise longue* which was as tidy as though it had never been slept on. No rumpled linen. No pillow tossed onto the floor and no six-foot-two, drop-dead gorgeous Italian scrunched up asleep.

No Candice either.

There were messages waiting for her the second she checked her phone, including a lengthy voicemail informing her that one of the kids had come down with hand, foot and mouth disease.

'Absolute nightmare!' Candice had sounded rushed and a little frantic on the voicemail. 'It's only a passing virus, and Toby will be over it in a couple of days, but of course Lucien is freaking out, so I've caught the first flight out, darling. Don't despair, though! I'll be back at the end of the week with the gang—and don't let that hunk of yours go anywhere! Lock him away if you have to! Everyone's dying to meet him!'

A long text message from her mother warned her that they, too, would be delaying their arrival so that they could lend a hand with two-year-old Jess while Candice was playing Florence Nightingale to her elder brother.

Probably a good idea to give you a little more private time with your young man! her mother had messaged, with a winking face next to it. So you can breathe a sigh of relief, darling.

With several skiing lessons booked for the day and behind time, Rosie raced through the room, flinging on the appropriate gear, and headed down, taking the short flight of stairs two at a time and screeching to a halt by the kitchen door. Matteo was in the kitchen. It was a little after eight, but he looked bright-eyed and bushy tailed, as though he had had a splendid night's sleep.

'Coffee?' He greeted her equably, shutting

the laptop which was in front of him on the kitchen table.

He was in a black polo-neck jumper and faded black jeans and he took her breath away.

Rosie blinked.

'How long have you been up?'

'A couple of hours. Hard to say.' He stood up and strolled towards the kettle to switch it on.

'Because you didn't manage to sleep well on the sofa?' Rosie inched into the kitchen, then told herself that it was ridiculous to feel uncomfortable in her own space. She needed to eat something before she shot out or she'd faint on the slopes. Her tummy was rumbling.

'It was a challenge,' he threw over his shoulder, 'But I've never been one to shy away from a challenge.'

Rosie had a vision of him on the *chaise longue*, half-naked, dwarfing it and yet accepting without complaint that that was his designated sleeping spot, and she felt it again—a stirring of tenderness that was disconcerting.

'Well, you're in luck,' she offered brightly. She headed for the bread bin and extracted a sandwich loaf that was, thankfully, fresh enough to pop into the toaster. 'Candice has had to rush off back to England because Toby has a virus.'

'Hand, foot and mouth,' Matteo murmured and Rosie looked at him with surprise.

'How do you know?'

'I was in the kitchen when she was heading out of here.'

'You were?'

'Like I said, sleeping was a challenge. I threw in the towel just in time to catch her before she left. She explained the situation.'

'Right.' Rosie hesitated as it dawned on her that there was no need for Matteo to stay at the chalet at all because there would be no one around to observe the lovers in action. He could return to the hotel and check himself in for however many nights before the family descended.

The chalet would feel very empty without him there, she thought, and just as quickly she banished that thought from her head. She had been in it on her own for weeks and it had been absolutely fine.

She had been ensnared by his personality and by the way he looked, and she had probably been a bit lonely without realising it. The instructors and all the young people working in the hotel were very friendly, and there was a brilliant social life on tap for anyone who wanted to dip in and out of it. There were always things happening in various groups in the evenings, depending on who happened to be working what shift. But many of her friends had paired up and she could only think that Matteo had lulled her into enjoying time with a guy on her own.

She had to remember that this was an artificial situation, though, and it annoyed her to feel that nudge of disappointment at the thought of him not being around.

'So I guess you've worked out what this means,' she said casually, offering him some toast, which he politely refused, even though he didn't appear to have eaten anything. There were no dirty plates to be seen and she had a feeling that he wouldn't have been meticulous about washing, drying and putting away anything he'd used.

'What?' Matteo strolled back to the chair and swivelled it so that he could watch her as she buttered her toast and then stood pressed against the counter, looking at him.

'You can return to the hotel and stay there until the family show up. I mean, Candice won't be here, and Mum and Dad are hanging back with her so that they can help with the kids while Toby is poorly. Emily and Rob will come later as well. It'll be a sudden onslaught but in the meantime there's no need for us to pretend because there will be no one around to see us.'

'No can do.'

'Sorry?' Rosie had bitten into her toast and she chewed it slowly. One slice. She'd be starving in an hour but thinking about all those career women Matteo was attracted to had got her thinking that she could do with shedding a few pounds and redirecting her love of chocolate into something else. Celery, perhaps.

'Bob and Margaret are still around,' Matteo elaborated. 'They're not staying at that hotel but they're there on a regular basis, enjoying one of the restaurants, drinking in one of the bars. There are only so many watering holes in this resort. Since the whole purpose of this arrangement was to convince them that we're the happy couple, it's hardly going to do if they spot me back at the hotel without you.'

'I hadn't thought of that,' Rosie admitted.

Which brought her to another realisation and that was that they would now be here, in this lodge together, without Candice and her entire family around to dilute the situation.

She dropped the toast into the bin and looked at him in consternation.

'Don't worry,' Matteo drawled, 'I'll make myself scarce.'

'That's not what I meant.'

'You have a face that's as transparent as a pane of glass. I have a mountain of work to get through, as it happens. This deal isn't the only thing on my plate at the moment. I'd planned on having time out at my villa in Venice to work solidly over the Christmas period, but now that that's been shot out of the water I'll have to get as much done as possible before your family get here.'

'At least you won't have to sleep on the sofa now.'

Matteo didn't say anything. The night had been a hideous lesson in physical discomfort and not because he was averse to sleeping on anything that wasn't a feather mattress. Growing up in a foster home, there had been no luxuries. He had become accustomed to a single bed with a mattress that seemed about as thick as a pound coin.

No, his discomfort had stemmed from the fact that he was way too big for such a delicate item of furniture.

And, as if that wasn't bad enough, he had been aware of her tossing and turning and then, at some point in the early hours of the morning, she had stumbled past him to go to the bathroom, mostly asleep, and after that getting back to sleep had been impossible.

Her body…

Even under the baggy tee shirt and the shapeless shorts he had glimpsed luscious curves that had sent an ache of desire straight to his groin. There was something about the light in this part of the world… The luminosity had penetrated through a crack in the curtain and as she had yawned her way past him, oblivious to his presence because she'd been dead to the world, the shadowy outline of her heavy breasts had been clearly visible.

His erection had been hard and immediate and he had had to suffer in silence, gritting his teeth while his imagination had taken flight.

Never had he felt such an intense craving to have any woman. It had shocked him and had been intensely unsettling because he hadn't been able to control his response.

If he'd managed half an hour's sleep for the entire night, he would have been surprised.

'You can have one of the guest bedrooms,' Rosie elaborated, breaking eye contact and then hovering. 'They're all made up and I can just replace the linen before the family arrive later in the week.'

She couldn't read his expression. If he always seemed to know what she was thinking because her face was 'as transparent as a pane of glass', then reading his thoughts was about as easy as groping a way forward in dense fog wearing a blindfold.

Right now, he was staring at her with hooded eyes, pinning her to the spot, even though she knew she had to run because her first client was in forty-five minutes.

'Good idea.' Matteo dropped his eyes and glanced at the laptop.

Her cue to go, Rosie thought. Enough small talk.

'I'll be on the slopes until this afternoon,' she said, edging past him to the door. 'And then I might go out with some of the gang this evening. So I won't be in your way.' They were talking to one another as though they were strangers and, although she knew that this was to be expected, given the fact that there were no witnesses in the vicinity to make judgement calls on their relationship, she couldn't help but miss the easy, teasing banter he was so good at whenever they were in public view.

'That's not going to work.' He caught her wrist, stopping her in her tracks.

A sizzle of electricity zapped through her and she froze. She wanted to shut her eyes because he was so clever at reading what was in her head and, right now, what was in her head was *I want this man.* She licked her lips but her mouth was dry and she couldn't seem to get any words out.

'Want to know why?' Matteo was gazing at her flushed face.

He rubbed the pad of his thumb absently over the softness of her inner wrist.

He could feel it. He could sense a physical response rippling through her, mirroring his.

This was playing with fire. He wasn't on the lookout for a relationship with anyone and certainly not with a woman who was as soft as meringue, no sharp edges, no defence barriers. Despite her wealthy background, she was so sweetly disingenuous that he would be crazy to go there.

He banked down the tide of images flooding his mind—pictures of her in bed naked, her plump, ripe body opening up for him.

He dropped her hand and sat back. 'You keep forgetting that we're supposed to be an item.'

'I don't think that Bob and Margaret will be partying at a club.'

'That's not the point. I expect glad tidings of our hot and heavy relationship have already reached the ears of most of your fellow clubbers. How's it going to look if you show up without me?'

'You could always come.'

'I'm not big into the club scene.'

Rosie distractedly rubbed her wrist where he had been touching it. 'Well, if everyone has heard all about us, and I honestly don't think that's the case, wouldn't it be a good idea if we were to do something outdoorsy?'

'Like gyrating on a dance floor at two in the morning?' He raised his eyebrows and Rosie shot him a reluctant grin.

'Everyone's too tired after being on the slopes all day to stay out until two in the morning. Gyrating.' Her smile widened. 'You sound like an old man.'

'I'm old compared to you,' Matteo told her irritably. 'I'm thirty-two. You're twenty-three. I've lived a life of responsibility. You've had the pleasure of doing just as you've always pleased without fear of consequences.' He paused, hating himself for wiping the easy smile off her face. 'It's what makes you who you are,' he said roughly. 'And that's no bad thing.'

'What do you mean?'

'I happen to like the way you approach life, as though each day is filled with the promise of something new and enjoyable.'

'It often is.'

'Is it?' He shrugged. 'You could be right but it's an optimism that usually gets ground into dust by the time reality takes over.'

'What do you mean by reality?'

'Work. Responsibility. Life in general.'

Rosie was so tempted to reach out and touch him. There was a vulnerability there and she was sure he wasn't even aware of it. He'd had a tough life and Lord only knew what sacrifices he had had to make along the way to get where he had.

'How did you get that scar?' she asked suddenly, expecting him not to offer a reply. She had done what he seemed constantly to be telling her not to do, namely push past his boundaries to invade his inner sanctum.

'Fight.' He smiled at her. 'I was a teenager at the time. Fights happened all the time. Someone had a knife and I got in the way of it.'

Her heart twisted and she backed towards the door. 'I should be going.'

'And I need to carry on with this work. What time are you wrapping it up with your lessons?'

'Last one at three.' Rosie knew she had to go and yet she didn't want to leave. Every small entry into his life felt magical. 'I need to go and buy some food,' she said, fidgeting. 'I've been lazy when it comes to buying stuff. It's easy to live off junk food because we get discounted prices at most of the cafés around here. One of the perks of being a ski instructor.'

'I noticed a lot of greenery,' Matteo remarked, enjoying the way she blushed, which was something that never failed to surprise him.

Rosie grimaced. 'I know. I always think that if I buy lots of lettuce and vegetables then I'm going to actually eat them. I should. I should never go anywhere near chips or burgers.'

'Why?'

'Can't you look at me and tell?' She laughed and then sobered up when her eyes collided with his and she saw that he wasn't laughing along with her.

His expression was…darkly hungry.

She shivered, a core of excitement reaching fever pitch as he continued to stare at her. By the time he lowered his gaze, her nerves were in crazy freefall and there was a heat between her thighs that made her want to rub them together.

'No, I can't, as a matter of fact,' Matteo intoned in a driven undertone that was quite unlike his usual lazy drawl.

'I'll see you later.' Rosie fled. Any longer

in his presence and she would start having heart palpitations. Could he see the effect he had on her? For a minute, just then, she had seen something in his eyes that had sent her pulses racing out of control. It was an attraction that had gone to her head like incense. He'd wanted her. She was sure of that.

Her mind was all over the place for the rest of the day. She waved at Bob and Margaret, who were trying out the slopes on their own. She discovered that Matteo had been right to think that news of their whirlwind romance had done the rounds. She had to think fast on her feet when questions were asked, building a picture of a relationship that had been clandestine. He'd been busy wrapping up a deal and she'd been busy with her ski lessons so they had enjoyed snatched time together and things had gone on from there.

Fortunately, due to the nature of the business, there were a lot of arrivals and departures and the few friends she had made who had been there as long as she had, doing the season, seemed to have such frenetic social lives after their duties were done, that they accepted her stammering explanations without delving too deep. Indeed, the thought of 'snatched time together' had struck her girl-friends as wonderfully exciting.

She was pleasantly tired by the time she saw off her last client. She was preparing to head back to the hotel to dump her stuff and change when she happened to glance to her left and there he was. Her heart skipped a beat, then it skipped a couple more as he made his way towards her, dressed in ski gear.

'I didn't think you skied,' she said breathlessly when he was standing in front of her.

She didn't think it was possible for anyone to look as good as he did in ski clothes. Aside from a thin orange strip along the top, he was dressed completely in black. His sunglasses were propped up and he hadn't shaved. She could make out the shadow of stubble on his chin.

At this hour, the slopes were emptying out, and from the resort below she could hear the distant strains of Christmas carols being played. Something about the stillness in the air seemed to trap the sound and hold it within the confines of the mountains rearing upwards, red, gold and white in the fading light.

'I don't.' He flashed her a smile. 'But you had a point when you said that some outdoor time together might be a good idea. Bought the gear, so here I am.'

'It's a little late…' Her skin was burning. 'But… I guess I could take you through the ropes. I mean, it's not as though you actually *want* to learn to ski.'

'Who knows?' Matteo murmured. 'With the right teacher, I might find I have untapped talent.'

Nervous as a kitten, and aware of her roundness thanks to the layers of ski gear, Rosie went through the paces with him.

'Feet together…take it slowly…keep the skis parallel… No, not quite like that. Here, let me show you. Don't forget to keep your eyes ahead! Are you scared of heights, by the way? Will you be spooked in the cable car?'

Rosie had never had so much fun. She was in her comfort zone and, as she laughed and tried to give him some handy tips, she caught herself telling him about when she had first taken to the slopes. It was the one thing she was better at than her sisters.

'They were clever,' she said, eyeing the distance between his skis, 'But I was always the sporty one.'

'I'm surprised you didn't think about making a career in it,' Matteo murmured.

'I'm a good skier,' Rosie laughed, 'But I'm not great enough to compete on an international level!'

'There's more to making a living in sport than practising it at an international level.'

This as they were making their way to the car, Matteo having managed to get hold of a personal driver to bring him down from the chalet.

Rosie paused for a fraction of a second and looked sideways at him.

'You mean like a sports teacher or something?'

'I mean...'

Matteo stopped and turned to look at her so that she was obliged to stop as well and stare up at him.

'The key thing is to find what you enjoy, because chances are you'll probably be good at it, and then with a favourable following wind you can make a career out of it.'

'You enjoyed making money and you were good at it so you made a career out of it?'

'I enjoyed the thought of being free. Money was just my passport to getting there. I've bought food.'

'Sorry?' Rosie's brain was lagging behind, dwelling on what he had said.

'Food. You said you needed. I've bought.'

Rosie felt a tingle of pleasure and for a few moments, a real sense of *contentment*. So this was what her sisters had, she thought with a pang. Someone to laugh with. Someone who bought food. Someone to open the car door for them.

She'd never had that.

This was just an illusion, and she didn't want to get sucked in, but it was hard when he was chatting to her as they slowly bumped their way back up to the chalet, which was in darkness by the time they got there.

Around them, the snow blanketed everything in white. The air was dry and cold. The house, however, was toasty warm as they entered, shaking off the snow and dumping coats, gloves, scarves and boots in the spacious cupboard by the front door.

The intimacy of their surroundings, just the two of them in the house, hit her with the force of a sledgehammer as they headed towards the kitchen, Matteo with two carrier bags in his hands.

He switched on lights as they went. He'd dumped the outer layers and was down to a thermal tee shirt that clung lovingly to his muscular torso.

'I'll just go and get changed...showered.' She was trailing behind him and she didn't give him time to look around, carolling gaily as she veered off to the staircase. 'And I'll pop a towel in the guest bedroom for you!'

Not that there's anything to worry about, she told herself. *He might have glanced at you with a show of interest but you're not his type. And he was the perfect gentleman last night. So making a point of telling him about the towel in the guest room is at best not very subtle and at worst a hint that you are downright terrified of sharing a bedroom with him when there's no sister conveniently lodged two rooms along.*

He had unpacked the carrier bags and the contents were laid out on the kitchen table in ceremonial fashion.

Rosie relaxed and grinned. She looked at what was there: tomatoes, some vegetables, duck eggs, an assortment of expensive pâtés, smoked salmon, various cheeses, an enormous box of the finest Swiss chocolates and a gateau that instantly made her mouth water.

'You don't need to watch what you eat.' Matteo followed her gaze to the gateau.

Rosie ignored him. She was so conscious of his presence that the hairs on her arms were standing on end.

'Duck eggs?' She held the blue box up to him.

'That was a mistake,' Matteo admitted.

'It's a very interesting assortment of food and thank you very much for going to the trouble of buying it. I'm not sure what I do with some of these ingredients. Maybe we should just have a salad for our supper.'

'There's bread,' Matteo informed her.

'I guess you don't cook at all?'

'I try and avoid it.' He found himself telling her that cooking had been *de rigueur* at the children's home when he'd been growing up and the very fact of that had instilled a healthy dislike for anything to do with pots, pans and food preparation.

What he didn't add was that he'd suffered from the realisation over the years that pots, pans and food preparation was what at least some women enjoyed doing in an attempt to whet his appetite for more than just the dishes they had lovingly prepared.

He watched as she fetched plates and busied herself opening the packets he had bought.

Did that count as food preparation? Nothing went into preparing a cold meal. It was ready in under half an hour and, looking at the spread, Matteo found himself wishing that he was about to eat something hot.

'Do you…enjoy cooking at all?' he queried, opening a bottle of wine.

It was a little after six. Early for supper, but it was dark outside, with flurries of snow reminding them of the time of year.

'I wouldn't say it's the love of my life.'

Rosie had tactfully stuck the gateau out of sight and she eyed the array of pâtés, cheeses and smoked salmon with a distinct lack of enthusiasm.

He'd obviously bought the sort of food he personally enjoyed.

'This wouldn't be your choice of food?' he quizzed and she looked at him sheepishly.

'I've always liked food that's a bit more... more...'

'Tasty?'

'This is all very good.'

'Wine will improve the flavours. Hang on for five secs.'

He disappeared and returned a few minutes later with two bottles of champagne.

'Forgot I bought these at the wine merchant.' He opened a bottle, found glasses, poured them a glass each and then returned to his seat.

Rosie was ashamed at just how good this felt, sitting here with this guy, eating a meal together, almost as though they weren't caught up in a charade, a game of make believe.

She was uneasily aware of how slender the line could be between reality and fantasy.

This felt real.

This felt more real than any of the passing connections she had ever made over the years with guys and she knew that it was because, very quickly and purely because of the situation, they had shared things with one another. He had shared his background—reluctantly, she knew—but still...

She had opened up to him, he had listened and somehow he had seen right into the very heart of her. That had promoted a feeling of... *closeness*.

The champagne was excellent. The best money could buy.

'I thought you had planned on working all day,' she said a little drowsily after champagne had been drunk and a dent made in the food.

'Bob and Margaret weren't available for comment.'

'I saw them on the slopes.'

'Did they approach you? Ask any questions?'

'They were too far away, but you were right about my friends seeming to know that we're involved. When this started, I had no idea that it would grow legs and start running away from me.' She sighed.

'Like I've said before...' Matteo fetched the gateau from where she had earlier hidden it behind the canisters of sugar and tea '...once you start lying, it's impossible to know where it's going to end up.'

'You must hate all of this.' She looked at the slab of cake in front of her and was indecently keen to tuck in. He produced two forks and gently pulled the plate between them.

'Care to share?'

Rosie's eyes widened. This felt truly intimate. They weren't touching one another— not even their forks touched!— yet as they at the slab of cake it felt weirdly *intimate*.

'You asked me whether I was hating all of this,' Matteo mused.

Her eyes were even more amazing up close, he distractedly found himself thinking. She couldn't quite meet his gaze and he knew, with the instinct of a man well versed in the way women reacted, that her response was a physical one. The champagne had relaxed her but she was still wary. He could sense it. He could almost smell it.

What would she do if he touched her? He found the thought of that so erotic that he had to grit his teeth together to ease the ache in his groin.

'You must be.'

'I should be,' he admitted, 'But I suppose that a change is as good as a rest.'

Rosie wanted to feel relieved at that, but

all she could think was, *You're enjoying the novelty of the situation. The novelty of being with someone like me. You've practically said so yourself.*

She didn't want to be a novelty but she wasn't going to give that away.

'I've put you in the room to the left of the staircase,' she said, changing the subject.

'There's a towel on the bed,' he added politely and she blushed.

'I'll tidy in the morning.' She staged a yawn which turned into the real thing. 'I'm exhausted. I always am in the evenings.'

'And yet you wanted to go clubbing tonight.'

'It was optimistic.'

'You don't have to try and run away from me,' he said kindly, which made her blush even more. 'As this evening has shown, we're two adults perfectly capable of passing the time of day together without any major disagreements. I'm going to stay up for a couple of hours, finish some emails. I think, if we can agree to stick to this routine until your family show up, life shouldn't be too overwhelming for us. Wouldn't you agree? And, as soon as my deal is signed, we can begin the process of...disentanglement.'

CHAPTER SIX

ROSIE STARED UP at the ceiling. She hadn't drawn the curtains and the silver light, the reflection of the moon shining down on endless white outside, illuminated everything in the bedroom.

This had always been her favourite time of the year—the run up to Christmas. The entire resort was a winter wonderland of tiny lights, Christmas trees and carols booming through the village, ratcheting up the excitement. Every year, the entire family would meet for a week at the chalet and it would mark the beginning to the countdown for them. They would put up a tree and the board games would come out. Family time.

She should have been alive with anticipation. Instead, she eyed the empty *chaise longue* and realised that her thoughts had been entirely occupied with Matteo.

At a little after one in the morning, he

would be sound asleep in a proper bed instead of lying awake, cramped and uncomfortable, on a sofa that she, inches shorter, would have found a challenge.

She thought about him bedding down without complaint and then waking up and busying himself on his computer at some ridiculously early hour in the morning, also without complaint. She knew that he would have spent his entire time at the chalet falling off a sofa in the middle of the night, perfectly accepting that, if that was his designated sleeping area, then so be it.

He had a childhood without any luxuries. As a small boy growing into a young man learning how to be tough and ambitious enough to ignore the siren call of violence—all that had prepared him to accept discomfort should it come his way. He might be worth billions now but she got the feeling that the past he seldom discussed was never forgotten.

Caught up in the fruitless exercise of thinking about him and trying to work him out, she finally decided to get out of bed and head down to the kitchen for something to eat.

She'd barely touched a thing all day and the gateau was beckoning.

The chalet was in darkness as she made

her way downstairs to the kitchen. Through the vast glass doors, she paused to take in the expanse of snowy white outside.

She shivered, feeling the chill, because the central heating had switched off at midnight. She should have slung on a bathrobe but satisfying her rumbling tummy had been far too pressing. Plus, she was sick of thinking about Matteo and then mentally asking herself why she couldn't put him out of her mind.

She'd managed to find every excuse under the sun for her relentless absorption with him, starting with *It's perfectly understandable, considering the way we were thrown together* then going on to *It would be unnatural for me not to think about him* and *There wouldn't be a woman alive who wouldn't be thinking of him if she was sharing a house with him... who could ignore someone who looks the way he does?*

She didn't bother turning on the kitchen light due to the unfounded suspicion that it might filter all the way upstairs to where Matteo was sleeping and alert him to the fact that there was someone downstairs.

As a consequence, she banged her foot against the edge of one of the chairs and hopped in agony for a few seconds until the pain subsided, then she opened the fridge and knelt down to inspect the contents.

She wanted to resist the cake but the alternative of eating whatever remained of the options Matteo had generously bought didn't tempt.

She reached out to cut a sliver of the gateau which Matteo had shoved in the fridge, not bothering to remove the knife he had earlier used to cut it, when the sound of his voice coming from behind her almost shocked her into having a heart attack.

With a yelp, she scuttled back and shot to her feet, heart pounding and mouth dry, and she spun round to look at him. The kitchen was still in darkness but to her horror that didn't last long because he banged on the switch and the room was flooded with light.

Never had Rosie felt more conscious of her state of undress. The tee shirt might be baggy but she was excruciatingly aware of the heavy weight of her bra-less breasts pushing against it, and her shorts were tiny. Way too small.

For a few seconds, she couldn't speak at all. She studied him, her thoughts in frantic disarray. She'd glimpsed him without a shirt on but this time… The man was *awesome*, she thought weakly, so very tall, so very well built. So very, very under-dressed.

Not only was he half-naked, but the safe option of tracksuit bottoms had been jettisoned in favour of boxers that revealed long, muscular legs and a stomach as flat as a wash board.

'What are you doing here?' she managed accusingly. In timely fashion, she reminded herself that this was, actually, *her* house and he was the guest so why should she feel as though she'd been caught red-handed stealing the family heirlooms? How was it that he somehow found it so effortless to exert control and thereby give the impression that he owned everything around him even if he didn't?

'I heard a noise.'

His voice was terse and, reading into that abrupt response, Rosie could only imagine his annoyance at finding his sleep disrupted yet again.

'I made sure to be quiet!'

'Noise travels around here.'

They stood and stared at one another and, suddenly conscious of herself, she crossed her arms over her breasts and was disconcerted when he followed that gesture. Was he trying to embarrass her on purpose? She swung away but the heavy silence was getting to her.

'I just came down to get something to drink.' She thought of the gateau and silently bid farewell to the chunk of lovely, comforting calories. 'Are you just going to stand there? I'm sorry if I woke you up. I had no idea I made any noise. I banged my toe but I didn't think I yelped loud enough for you to hear.'

'I might as well get myself something to drink as well now that I'm down here,' Matteo muttered, moving forward with the quiet grace of a panther to open the fridge and extract two bottles of water, one of which he handed to her.

Instead of walking towards the door, he remained standing next to her, unsettling in his masculine beauty, holding her transfixed gaze until her legs began to feel wobbly.

Water in hand, she began backing away towards the door, eyes on him the whole time.

'I thought someone had broken in.' He moved towards her, his voice lacking its usual cool self-control. He sounded as though he needed to clear his throat.

'That's rare over here.' Rosie breathed, watching wide-eyed as he stopped in front of her. There was nowhere else to go so she remained where she was, staring up at him and trying hard to play it cool when her pulse was racing and her heart was slamming against her rib cage. 'You could sleep with the doors open and no one would break in.'

'You have the most amazing eyes,' Matteo murmured.

'Matteo...'

'I like it when you say my name in that breathy little voice.'

'Matteo, don't.'

'I'm not doing anything.'

But he was. Right now, he was. He was lifting one hand to sift it through her wildly tousled fair curls. Her mouth ran dry. She badly wanted to touch him but she had no idea how this kind of game went. He traced the outline of her mouth with his finger, then cupped the side of her face and stared at her for a long moment until her head was swimming.

'What's going on?' she whispered.

'As if you don't know.' He laughed softly. 'Haven't I told you how sexy I find you? I'm attracted to you, *mia bellissima*. And it's mutual, or are you going to deny it?'

'You're a good-looking man,' Rosie prevaricated.

'Would you like this good-looking man to kiss you?'

Rosie nodded, an unfamiliar, but powerful heat running through her body.

He lowered his head and the kiss...took

her to heaven and left her there. His mouth was cool and when he inserted his tongue she reached up on tiptoe and wrapped her hands around his neck to pull him down closer to her.

A little groan escaped her. Her breasts felt heavy, her nipples sensitised to the point of painful. She ached for him and curved her body in a wriggling movement that invited him to slip his hand underneath the tee shirt.

For a second, Rosie stilled, but only for a second. He brushed her waist with his hand while he continued to ravish her with a never-ending kiss. Of its own volition, her body seemed to have closed what little gap there had been between them.

Lost in a world of sensation, and feeling as though her body was alive for the very first time, Rosie only realised that he had gently propelled her towards the kitchen table when she bumped against the edge of it.

He eased her apart from him and kept his eyes locked to hers when he began to slip the tee shirt up.

Mesmerising eyes, Rosie thought. Bottomless and fringed with indecently long lashes. Inch by inch the tee shirt was lifted until she was standing in front of him, her breasts exposed.

She felt a surge of feminine power when his nostrils flared as he looked down at her body.

She reached behind to prop herself against the table, clutching the edge with her hands and leaning ever so slightly back so that her body was inclined towards his, towards his heated, appreciative gaze.

He cupped her breasts in his hands and massaged them, simultaneously rolling his thumbs over the stiffened peaks. The groans became restless whimpers.

She wanted much more than this.

She wanted everything.

And suddenly, she realised that she was never going to get what she wanted. She was never going to get anything deep or significant with this guy.

Was this her?

Everything that was rooted in principle and tradition flared into life and she caught his hands in hers and looked at him with troubled eyes.

'I'm not sure I can do this,' she said on a miserable sigh, and just like that he dropped his hands and she lowered the tee shirt. 'I know we're adults, and this is what adults do when they fancy one another, but I'm not sure this is…*me*.'

'You're not...sure?'

'I've only had one serious relationship, Matteo, and that was a long time ago and it didn't end well. I thought we were going somewhere, heading somewhere, but it turned out that he was using me. Maybe not to start with, maybe there was something genuine there at the beginning, but in the end the family money, the trust fund...it all meant more to him.'

'What does a relationship you had years ago have to do with this?'

There was genuine bewilderment in his voice, and that threw her, because in her head the two seemed to be tied together, but why? Did he have a point? Did one bad relationship have to influence every relationship thereafter?

Confusion seeped in. She wondered what, exactly, she was looking for. Permanence? Of course, she came from a secure and loving background. Her parents had been with one another for a lifetime and beyond. But did that mean that the only route open to her was with a guy she would end up marrying and settling down with?

What about the benefits of just having fun? Despite all the adventures she had had on her travels, hadn't she been at pains to avoid the greatest adventure of all—getting involved with someone? Opening up to them, whatever the outcome? Relationships had lasted five minutes because split decisions had been made that he wasn't the one.

'If you have to turn this into a drama in five acts, then maybe I misjudged things.' Matteo's voice had cooled and he stepped away from her, leaving behind an icy-cold void. 'I'm sorry.' His eyes were as dark and as deep as a glacier.

'Matteo...'

'I'm going to head up, Rosie. I'll see you in the morning.'

He spun round on his heels and soundlessly left the kitchen. In his wake, she subsided onto one of the kitchen chairs and thought, but she couldn't make sense of any of her thoughts. Matteo came from a different world from hers and not just in the material sense. He was hard, tough, had dragged himself up by the bootstraps and had battled whatever adversities he had faced to do it. He had money now but he had learnt from his experiences and now lived his life accordingly.

Something inside her shifted, adjusted and settled into another place and she began heading up the stairs, straight to the bedroom where he had been put.

He was up, lounging on the bed with his hands clasped behind his head, staring at the ceiling.

She could see him in the silver light filtering through the windows because, like her, he hadn't drawn the thick curtains, preferring the distant view of craggy, soaring, snowy mountains.

'I know I'm soft,' Rosie began, walking into the room, fired up.

'What the…?'

'Just let me say what I have to say!'

'Go to bed, Rosie. I'm not in the mood for a raging sermon from you. You don't have to justify your decisions to me.'

'I know I'm soft. I've been spoilt. I don't take anything for granted, believe me I don't, but that doesn't mean that I'm not aware of all the privileges I've grown up with. Maybe you think that that has something to do with me wanting the fairy-tale ending when it comes to romance and you could be right. My big relationship ended with a whimper but don't you dare tell me that you don't see what that has to do with anything.'

Matteo had sat up and she was propelled towards the bed—towards *him*.

Against the white bed linen, his burnished gold body, the deep, rich colour of someone in whom exotic genes ran like a thread of gold, was a powerful, lithe reminder of his intense masculinity.

'We're *all* affected by our pasts.' She perched on the edge of the bed and stared at him. His face was in shadow but she knew that he was watching her. She just didn't know what he was thinking, but when did she ever? 'You are. You haven't had *my* past, but you're as affected by yours as I am by mine. Our pasts are what shape us, and I'm not going to have you tell me that you have no idea what one broken relationship has to do with anything. You don't let anyone into your life because of what you went through. You don't like Christmas, and there would be a reason for that somewhere, buried in your past. So, I was hurt once and I never want to be hurt again.'

'You've said your piece and I've listened, Rosie. You should go to sleep now.'

'I'm attracted to you.'

'Don't go there,' Matteo warned in a dangerously low voice. 'I don't like game playing.'

'Isn't that what we've been doing ever since we met one another?'

'Wrong phrasing. I don't want any woman thinking she has to play games with me.'

'I'm not,' Rosie told him abruptly. She felt a surge of empowerment from her decision taken with eyes wide open. 'We're attracted to one another, and it's not about whether this will lead anywhere or not. I *know* it's not going anywhere. I *know* I'm not your type and you're not mine. So I'm not going to be hurt. I'm going to have fun.'

'What are you saying?'

Reckless daring swept through her in a *now or never* moment as she pulled the tee shirt over her head and stood in front of him, fighting hard not to succumb to crippling self-consciousness.

He wasn't saying anything but his silence wasn't the silence of someone politely about to channel her out of the bedroom and that was encouraging. The silence was still and thick with electricity.

She stepped out of the rest of her clothes and for a few seconds squeezed her eyes shut.

'Come.'

One word and it was enough.

This was a situation far removed from both their comfort zones and, if she only subliminally recognised the danger that particular novelty carried, then Matteo was all too aware of it.

Novelty, in his rarefied world, was a scarce

commodity. He'd suffered the indignities of being the poor kid at a rich school, where he'd earned a scholarship to board at the age of thirteen. He'd learned the hard way to ignore every single thing that wasn't worth taking on board and that had included all manner of insults and verbal abuse. Ambition, an intellect that was in the stratosphere, an ability to take risks…all of those things had propelled him onwards and upwards, and he had had no time to relax…until now.

He'd made it. He had more money than most people could dream of. Enough to turn his back on work and live on a beach, drinking cocktails, for the rest of his life. But, in the cold light of day, there was a part of him that acknowledged that he was *bored*. What else was there to get? He could have anything he wanted. Any *woman* he wanted. All those top-notch career women, brainy, beautiful and independent, would still do anything he asked. He could read it in the way they looked at him, the way they listened to what he said, even in the way they sometimes played hard to get.

But she was right. His past had made him the person he was today, locked in a controlled world where he called the shots and there were no unpleasant surprises on any front—material or emotional.

Then into his safe, predictable and obscenely wealthy life this woman had parachuted and she was nothing like any woman he'd met before.

On paper, she made no sense. Life had taught him to walk away from poor little rich girls with their aggrieved air of entitlement and their healthy trust funds. He had no time for anyone for whom life was easy. His admiration was reserved for those who had faced at least some of the tough mountains he had had to conquer. Most of the women he had dated had worked hard to climb the ladder of success. They had gone beyond the call of duty and battled in a world that was largely, and stupidly, male dominated. Some had made marks that would live on after them.

There was no way that Rosie Carter could possibly qualify for any of those categories. She came from a privileged, private-school background but she surprised him at every turn. It had taken guts to do what she had just done. She was a breath of fresh air and he wanted her more than he had ever wanted any woman in his entire life.

Temptation had never looked so irresistible. Rosie pushed her fair, curly hair behind her ears and stared at him. Her heart was pounding like a sledgehammer in her chest. It was chilly in the room, but her body was on fire, as if someone had taken a match and lit a bonfire under her feet.

He flung back the duvet, inviting her in, and she could see that he was completely naked. Her mouth went dry and the fire burning up inside her went from sizzling to molten.

She stifled a groan as their bodies met and she felt the push of his erection against her.

'I don't get it,' she whispered. 'I can't seem to help myself.'

'What's going on here,' he said, 'Is something that neither of us had banked on. There's a chemistry here that defies logic. Like you said, I'm not the sort of guy you're accustomed to dating and the same goes for me with you. Sexual attraction has a way of defying logic.'

Rosie's breath hitched in her throat at the feel of his hand gently smoothing her thigh, circling just by her crotch. She moaned softly and lay back, eyelids fluttering shut, parting her legs just a bit more so that he could nudge the dampness between her thighs with his knuckles. It was gentle, seductively rhythmic, and her breathing quickened in response.

'You have no idea how much you turn me on,' Matteo rasped shakily, tugging her so that he could plant a series of kisses on the side of her neck. 'You're breathtakingly sexy.'

'So are you.' Rosie's eyes were hot and drowsy as she caressed the side of his face before cradling the back of his head with her hand and pulling him into a kiss that melted everything in her body. His mouth was cool and firm and the feel of their tongues meshing was indescribable.

It was a kiss she never wanted to end. She curved into him, her body pale and smooth in the dim light.

He didn't talk but he didn't have to. His appreciation of her body was in the way he touched her and the hot fire in his amazing eyes.

He bent to suckle one throbbing nipple, drawing it deep into his mouth, tasting and feasting while sensations spiralled in her, making her wriggle and writhe underneath him.

She'd never wanted anyone so badly. Had never come close.

Her body was flushed and tingling all over when he eventually straightened. The contrast in their colouring was dramatic—she so pale, he burnished gold. He stepped off the bed and she could see that he was rummaging in his wallet for a condom. He dropped it on the wooden table by the side of the bed and looked at her with brooding intensity for a few silent seconds.

'What are you doing?'

'I'm looking.' He held himself in his hand and absently pleasured himself for a few seconds.

.Without thinking, she reached up. On cue, he stepped towards her, and she traced the sinewy ridges of his erection with a trembling finger, starting at the base and working slowly to the tip, which she circled until his fists were clenched at his sides in an attempt to maintain some semblance of self-control.

He finally caught her wrist and breathed deeply.

'Any more,' he said roughly, 'And I'll come—and when I come I want to be deep inside you.'

He slowly joined her back on the bed but, instead of kissing her, he lowered himself to her belly and kissed her there, along her rib cage, while she trembled under the caress.

He circled her belly button with his tongue and then darted it into the sensitive hollow there before moving down lower to her panties, in an intimacy she had never experienced before.

She fought against snapping her legs shut and, as if sensing the impulse, he placed both flattened palms on the inside of her thighs, holding her open for him.

That very first sensation as he began to nuzzle the dampness between her legs was electrifying.

She wanted to thrash around, arch up against his questing mouth. The breath caught in her throat and then what emerged was a guttural groan of utter pleasure as he began working his tongue along the slippery groove that shielded her clitoris.

When he delicately began tracing the delicate, throbbing bud of her clitoris, she fisted her hands and moaned against her knuckles. It was exquisite. Transporting. She began to move against his mouth, finding his rhythm and matching it to her own.

She couldn't stop the shattering force of her orgasm. It ripped into her and she spasmed against his mouth, stifling her cries of pleasure, reaching to curl her fingers into his hair so that she could press his face harder between her quivering thighs.

The strength of her orgasm left her weak,

flushed and drowsy and it took her a few moments before she surfaced.

'I'm sorry,' she uttered, dismayed, but he was smiling.

'For what? Enjoying yourself?'

'This wasn't what was supposed to happen.'

She wrapped her arms around him and buried her face against the side of his neck because there was something shockingly intimate in what had just taken place, at how her body had reacted.

The freedom she had felt at that moment of coming made her feel as though her soul had opened up.

Suddenly, she wanted *more*, but she wasn't too sure what.

She tentatively rested her hand on his lean, firm buttocks, then stroked him. He flipped her over and positioned her so that she was lying on top of him. Like this, his pulsing manhood against her was a powerful reminder of the chemistry uniting them against all odds. She had just had an explosive orgasm, and her body wanted a repeat performance, but this time she wanted him inside her, moving deep and hard.

X-rated thoughts made her feel faint. She arched up so that her heavy breasts dangled invitingly close to his mouth and their eyes tangled in the subdued darkness.

'Very sexy,' Matteo murmured shakily and, when he contained her breasts between his hands, squashing them gently together, he couldn't contain a groan of utter pleasure.

That did something to her. A strain of wanton recklessness that she had never known she possessed sizzled through her with lightning speed.

She angled her body lower and levered her nipple into his mouth, propping herself up so that he could suckle on it while she watched. It was erotic, giddily so. Very slowly, she began to move against him, sinuously and seductively, inching left to right, and then in small, circular motions that heightened his responses and brought a flare of scorching lust to his eyes.

In the end, he couldn't stand it any longer He groaned, pulled her down to him and then kept completely still for a few seconds, breathing himself back into a place of some self-control.

'I need to be inside you,' he said hoarsely. 'You're driving me crazy.'

That was music to Rosie's ears. She felt as though she was waking up, stepping into the real world, for the very first time in her life.

She watched him heave himself off the bed, every movement clumsy and uncoordinated, testimony to the fact that, whatever he was feeling, it had complete control over him. He donned protection, easing the condom over his erection, taking time because of his size.

She was aching for him…couldn't stay still. She whimpered as he levered himself over her and then the whimper turned into a cry of intense satisfaction when he finally pushed into her.

He moved slowly at first, driving deeper into her, and then faster, holding them both at bay until, on one final thrust, he groaned and she felt him swell inside her. Indescribably turned on, she wrapped her legs around him and let wave after wave of pleasure surge over her. Their bodies were as one. She could never have imagined feeling so close, so united, with anyone.

Spent, her breathing took its time returning to normal, but then she sighed happily and wriggled against him.

Her head was against his chest and Matteo trailed his fingers through her hair, sifting free the tangles. Her warm breath puffed against him. She had one thigh across his and he felt her dampness. She was so soft…sexy curves and bountiful breasts…with an eagerness that was as sweet as the summer sun.

For the first time in his life, Matteo felt exposed. Had sex ever been that good? He had only just come down from a high and he wanted to go there again. He had no inclination to head straight for the shower. His mind wasn't moving on to other things. There was no creeping urge to free himself from the presence of another body sharing his bed.

Disquieted, he eased himself back with a frown and lay flat to stare up at the ceiling and, immediately sensing the shift in atmosphere, she pulled back as well.

The urge to get her back close to him, pressed against him, was strong but Matteo resisted, asserting control over a situation that seemed to have pulled against the reins and galloped off in directions unknown.

'I know you're going to say that this was a mistake,' Rosie began and he turned to look at her.

Matteo thought that she would do well to steer clear from mind reading because she couldn't have been further from the truth. If what had just happened between them was a mistake, then he had been well and truly caught in the grip of it, and furthermore wanted a repeat performance. What was going on? He had encouraged the situation. He would be the first to admit that. He had wanted her and he had finally succumbed, had laid his cards on the table, made a pass, did what came so naturally to him. He just hadn't predicted that their love-making would be so explosive. Disturbingly so.

'You have no idea what I'm going to say,' he managed.

'I can tell from your silence...'

'I wouldn't call it a mistake.'

'Then what would you call it?'

'A complication. I'd call it a complication, and now we need to think about what we're going to do about it...'

CHAPTER SEVEN

'WE DON'T HAVE to do anything about it,' Rosie said, mouth down-turned as she stared at her pale hands clasping her knees. 'You're right. It shouldn't have happened. These things do.'

But never, Rosie thought with a rapidly beating heart, *to her*. In *her* world she'd become friends with some guy, there would be a little bit of flirting, but nothing, in the end, would lead anywhere—because sooner or later she would lose interest and there had never been the driving physical need she had felt with Matteo.

Nothing like it.

In her world, nothing had ever happened. No lights had been ignited. No breathless excitement. No *wanting* so big that it drowned out all the little voices urging caution.

In *her* world, she thought, life had never really been lived.

And, now that she had tasted what living to the full felt like, it was going to be snatched out of her grasp, because what had been momentous for her had been routine for him.

'Not to me,' Matteo said seriously. He reached to clasp her hands and held them in his, and Rosie relaxed a little.

The last thing she wanted was for him to see how vulnerable she felt.

'What do you mean?' she asked cautiously.

'I mean...' Matteo raked his fingers through his hair and frowned, as though trying to get his thoughts in order. 'Life doesn't spring surprises on me.'

'What, never?'

'Never.' He paused and looked at her. 'We don't come from the same world,' he said flatly. 'I may have as much money as I could ever want now, but life is more than just the sum total of the present. Life is a series of small sums, adding up to the person we eventually become, to the way we deal with what life throws at us. You have always lived your life in the exclusive conclave of the wealthy. You, I am sure, have always been open to surprises because there was always a comfort blanket waiting to break your fall if the surprise didn't turn out to be a good one.'

Matteo felt safe saying that. Black and

white he could deal with. Grey occupied unknown territory and something inside resisted the threat of dealing with it.

Rosie blushed. 'That's not fair.'

'No, I don't suppose it is, but you can see what I'm getting at.'

'Yes. You're going to tell me that I'm not the sort you're attracted to because I don't have a hot-shot career in the City. Not everyone does and hot-shot careers aren't what they're cracked up to be. Have you any idea how stressed out some of those women are?'

'Stress can be an issue,' he murmured.

'I would rather be outside teaching sport than cooped up in a building popping antidepressants because I'm finding it hard to deal with the anxiety.' Rosie wasn't going to roll over and play dead.

Matteo grinned, eyebrows raised, expression so unconsciously sexy that it was making the blood in her veins hot with a resurgence of desire.

How was it possible to be so fiercely turned on by someone who was in the process of giving her her walking papers because she wasn't suitable? But she was and she shifted uncomfortably.

'You don't have to bang the drum for people who don't wear power suits.' He shrugged.

'My point is that neither of us anticipated this but it doesn't mean that...'

'That?'

'That I didn't want it to happen and don't want it to happen again.'

'What are you saying?' She licked her lips and registered the way his eyes followed that tiny movement. With hunger. The same hunger she was feeling inside her. Like a match set to tinder, it ignited a series of popping explosions inside her.

Matteo Moretti, self-made billionaire, had come to this five-star Italian ski resort for one reason and one reason only—to close a deal that meant a lot to him.

He hadn't banked on suddenly having his life go off the rails because of her. One minute he had been politely shaking hands with his prospective clients, the next minute he had been on the back foot trying to justify bad behaviour of which he wasn't guilty. He'd been forced into a situation not of his making because of circumstances he could never have predicted. He wanted to do what it took to make his deal happen, and what that took involved a pretend romance with the least likely woman on the planet, as far as he was concerned.

So far, so bad, but on top of that here they

were. Unlikely lovers. Had she expected that? She'd certainly acknowledged his massive sex appeal but no way had she projected that thought further into the realms of actually making love.

Now he was being honest and telling her like it was. He'd enjoyed what had happened between them. He wanted more, but there were a lot of conditions attached to that and a lot of sub-clauses he wanted her to understand.

She wasn't his type. She led the sort of privileged lifestyle he had commandeered for himself and made his own but his respect was reserved for people who had fought their way up, as he had. He dated bankers and lawyers and she was an intellectual lightweight—she would be the first to admit it. She'd never been in the league of either of her sisters and she'd packed in trying to be years ago, roughly around the time when her form teacher had kindly suggested to her parents that she focus on sport and arts and crafts.

Rosie was at a crossroads. Back away and put that one night down to a fantastic experience, never to be repeated, or else do what he wanted to do and prolong that one night for just a tiny bit longer, until the charade was over and they went their separate ways. An amicable break-up, initiated by her, between two people who had fallen for each other in haste but had thankfully come to their senses before any permanent damage could be done.

In a flash, she trawled back through the years and could see that her rebellious behaviour, her travelling and changing jobs and all those brief, barely notable liaisons with unsuitable boys had been as predictable as the rising and setting of the sun. He'd been right when he'd said that a comfort blanket of financial and emotional security had made all her choices safe. None of his choices had ever been safe. He would always have had a lot to lose and that dangerous edge to him was so appealing.

For the first time in her life, she knew in her heart that to follow him to where he was now pointing would be the most challenging and exciting choice she would ever make. It was so far out of her comfort zone that she had no idea where it might lead.

Not together in some happy-ever-after scenario, was the thought that flashed through her head. *But would she still be in one piece...?*

'I know what you're saying,' she said in a rush. 'You don't want this to be a one-night stand but you want me to remember that it isn't going to be anything more than a brief fling.'

Matteo was looking at her carefully, his silver eyes hooded and watchful.

He was waiting for her to accept his proposal on his terms. No involvement.

'I'm not looking for any kind of relationship,' he told her flatly. 'Here we are and the sex was fantastic.'

'Have you *ever* been interested in having a relationship with someone?' Rosie asked with genuine curiosity.

'That's not on my radar.'

'Why?'

'Why? Because everything I've ever seen has taught me that romance and all the fairytale nonsense that accompanies it comes with a lamentably short lifespan. I prefer to hedge my bets where the odds are better for a successful outcome.'

'Making money.'

'Works for me.' His voice hardened and she was reminded of the gaping chasm between them.

Common sense was making her question how she could be attracted to a guy who was so brutally honest when it came to his intentions.

'We *are* going to be stuck together for a

few days more…' she began, yielding to the riptide of physical attraction.

Matteo's slow smile was the smile of the victor and he angled her so that their bodies were pressed together, stomach to stomach, her generous breasts squashed against his muscled chest.

She rested the palm of her hand firmly on his chest, just in case he thought that she was a rag doll, helpless and obedient. He was so staggeringly sexy, so stupidly good-looking, that she knew without a shadow of a doubt that women would trip over themselves to get an invite into his bed. 'And I get it. You don't have to warn me that you're not interested in a relationship with me. I'm not interested in any kind of relationship with you either.'

'So you're not into flowers, chocolates and romance?'

'I never said that. I'm just not interested in flowers, chocolates and romance *with you*.'

'I like that we're on the same page.'

'I can keep things separate,' she assured him, ignoring the shadow of doubt that whispered over her skin. 'Business is the fact that we have to present a certain front for a short while, and pleasure is…'

'What happens when the lights go off?' He traced the side of her cheek with his finger and she shivered, eyelids fluttering, body responding instantly to that gently, teasing caress. 'Or on...' he murmured seductively. 'Either way works for me.'

'What works for me,' Rosie told him, 'Is some sleep. I have to teach tomorrow and then in the afternoon there's a little Christmas thing for the kids at the resort.'

'A Christmas thing?' He frowned.

She remembered what he'd said about Christmas not being his thing, but it was *her* thing, and if he was to convince her sister that they were an item, and by extension her family who would be trooping over only days from now, he would at least have to pretend to enjoy the festive season.

'It's no big deal.' She shrugged. 'You don't have to come but it'll only be for an hour or so. My sister will be there and some of her friends.'

'I'm getting the picture. If I'm a no-show, doubts might start being cast on our love-struck, whirlwind relationship.' He shrugged. 'I think it's fair to say that the rewards when we get back to this bed will more than compensate for sitting through some festive carols...'

Matteo was unprepared for what awaited him later that evening. Rosie had disappeared to work promptly at ten, and he had closed the door and settled down to make full use of the seldom used office, but having set up camp he instantly realised that his focus wasn't totally what it should have been.

Responding to emails had taken longer than usual because he caught himself sitting back, chair pushed away from the desk, contemplating what the night held in store for him. He'd spent a lifetime winning at everything he undertook but this victory felt so much sweeter.

The woman had cast a spell. He'd told her things he'd never divulged to anyone else. He'd opened up in ways that were hardly earth-shattering in the great scheme of things, and pretty routine by most people's standards, but which were earth shattering *for him*. He was a man who never confided. There had never been any pillow talk. People had no right of entry to his private life, he had long concluded, and if along the way some might have been offended by the rigidity of his Keep Out signs, then he really didn't care.

But there was something about this woman...

He told himself that there had been a perfectly good reason to confide in her. They were supposedly in a serious relationship and he had found himself on the back foot, having to explain his intentions to her sister, to his clients and to her family when they rolled up. It made sense to fill her in on some of his background, if only for the sake of verisimilitude, and it wasn't as though he was ashamed of his past. It had made him the pillar of strength and single-minded purpose that he was, hadn't it?

That said, Matteo was uneasily aware that something had shifted inside him, although he couldn't quite put a finger on what exactly, or how seismic the shift was.

So it was a relief when, at a little after four, the time arranged to meet Rosie at the resort for festive fun, he abandoned his work and headed down to the five-star hotel.

He smiled when he remembered her earnest attempt to teach him how to ski. He figured there was no harm in having another lesson.

He took a taxi to the resort and was deposited at a scene of outlandish Christmas extravagance.

At least, as far as he was concerned.

For a few seconds, he stood and stared. The hotel was lit up with hundreds of thousands of lights. He thought that up in the heavens, a million light years away, some alien life forms would be wondering what the hell was going on down here on planet Earth because the light display would surely be visible from outer space. The glittering, twinkling lights were weirdly hypnotic against the soft fall of snow and the whiteness of the landscape.

There were flurries of people everywhere, entering, leaving, skis on shoulders, holding hands with their kids. Evidently, this was something of a popular tradition. He steeled himself to sit through whatever lay ahead, now that he was here, and dialled Rosie's mobile, which remained unanswered.

Someone jostled him from behind, laughing and wishing him season's greetings in Italian, and that galvanised him into joining the throng of people heading into the hotel.

His irritation levels were rising fast when he heard her from behind, and he swung round.

He had already concluded that coming here had been an error of judgement. He was uncomfortable with the chaos and the over-the-top Christmas decorations everywhere. He had somehow expected the festivities to be of a more sombre nature: a choir singing carols in a dining area cleared of tables, perhaps. Instead…

He was scowling as he swung round, already formulating how he could politely make his excuses and clear off back to the chalet and wait for Rosie there.

And there she was. Santa's Christmas helper—red-and-white-striped tights, knee-high black boots with red *faux* fur at the top, small mistletoe-green dress with matching red fur swishing round the hem and at the cuffs of the sleeves, and a jaunty red-and-green hat set at an angle under which her flyaway, curly blonde hair peeped out with unruly abandon.

His breath caught in his throat and he stared.

'You're...' he managed to say hoarsely, raking his fingers through his hair.

'An elf. I know.' Rosie laughed but she was blushing madly because he was making no attempt to conceal the hot appreciation in his eyes. She'd seen him standing there, so perfectly still and watchful while the crowds swarmed around him. His tension was evident in his rigid posture and, from behind, she had pictured him frowning, irritable, about to glance at his watch. All of those things.

The guy didn't do Christmas, and why would he when he had spent his childhood in a children's home? Yes, maybe there had been the usual celebrations there, but without family it would still have been a lonely time. She hadn't thought but, hot and bothered as she was by the way he was looking at her, she still managed to reach out to circle his arm with her hand and draw him away from the centre of the vast lobby where pandemonium reigned.

'I'm sorry,' was the first thing she said when they were in a corner which was relatively quiet and she could hear herself think. There was still too much hubbub around. She pulled him into one of the smaller rooms where Tim, one of the managers, held his briefings with the ski instructors every morning. She shut the door and turned to face him, back to the door.

'I'm sorry,' she repeated quietly, and Matteo frowned, then strolled towards the large rectangular desk and perched against it, long legs extended and linked at the ankles.

He was such a specimen of pure physical perfection, she thought helplessly. Black jeans, black ribbed jumper, black coat—inappropriately non-waterproof and so stupidly elegant. He removed the coat and dumped it on the desk behind him.

'What are you sorry about?'

'I shouldn't have asked you to come here.'

'I don't recall you asking and, just for the

record, I'm not in the habit of doing what other people tell me to do unless I want to. I'm here because I chose to come.'

'But you don't do Christmas.' She didn't back away from saying what was on her mind, doggedly bypassing the uninviting expression on his face. 'And this is the most Christmassy a place could get. You must hate it. I don't suppose,' she continued, tenderness sprouting shoots as she thought of him young and alone in a home without the jolly family chaos she had had growing up, 'That Christmas was great in…er…when you were growing up.'

'Is that the sound of you feeling sorry for me?'

'Yes. Is that a crime?' Rosie tilted her chin at a stubborn angle and folded her arms.

'You always say what's on your mind, don't you? I'm here, and I'll bet Bob and Margaret are somewhere in the throng of people. No need to pull out the sympathy card.' He thawed and appreciatively ran his eyes over her. 'I like the outfit, by the way.'

Rosie reddened. 'I don't think elf outfits were designed for my particular shape, but I promised. Barry, the guy in charge of the entertainment over Christmas, has always been good to me.'

'Good? In what way *good*?'

He looked at her with sudden, brooding intensity. He had no idea from where it had come, but out of the blue a spark of white-hot jealousy had suddenly ripped into him. He thought of her warmth and her voluptuous sexiness curling against his body and all thoughts of her sharing herself with someone else, anyone else, sent his brain into instant meltdown.

It was disconcerting, bewildering. He had never considered himself to be a jealous person. A man who was jealous was a man who lacked the sort of iron-clad self-assurance which he possessed in bucket-loads.

Never had he gone out with any woman and paid the slightest bit of attention to lovers she might have had in the past or, for that matter, to any men who might have come on to her in his presence. He had always had the supreme confidence of a man who knew in his gut that he had everything it took to keep a woman glued to his side for just as long as he wanted her there.

Why would he ever have been jealous of any other man? Emotions, like every other aspect of his life, were there to be controlled. A childhood in which control had always lain in the hands of other people, with rules and regulations there to be obeyed, had resulted in an adulthood where he made his own rules and regulations and was controlled by no one.

And a childhood devoid of the love of a parent, where efficiency had come a poor second to love and affection, had nurtured in him a healthy wariness when it came to his heart and handing it over to anyone. Frankly, that was something he would never do.

So, with those two factors firmly in place, why the attack of irrational jealousy?

'You're not *jealous,* are you?'

Matteo lowered his fabulous eyes for a split second and, when he next met her headlong stare, his expression was as controlled as always.

'I don't do jealousy.'

'There's an awful lot of things you don't do.'

'I do sexy, little red-and-green elf outfits.'

'If you don't *do* jealousy, then why does it matter how Barry is good to me?'

Rosie folded her arms and gazed at him, mouth set. She had never been one to let anything go. Yes, she was non-confrontational when it came to her family, because the path of least resistance had always been the most convenient one to take, but in all other respects she could be as stubborn as a mule when it came to getting answers to questions she asked. And Matteo Moretti seemed to have an amazing knack when it came to arousing her curiosity. Five minutes in his company and she could feel a thousand questions piling up in her head.

She imagined him jealous of her—possessive, guarding her with caveman-like, finger-crooking ownership—and, much as her logical brain instantly revolted against the sexist image, a very feminine part of her twisted with simmering excitement.

'You're doing it again,' Matteo said with exasperation. He shook his head. 'Has it occurred to you that, if we're supposed to be the loved-up couple, the last thing I need is an intrusive old flame entering into the picture and trying to pick up where he may have left off a couple of months ago?'

Simmering excitement was replaced by full-blown anger and Rosie took a step closer to him.

'First of all,' she hissed, glaring, 'How dare you imply that I'm the sort of person who lets a guy *pick up where he left off* as though I have no mind of my own? Do you honestly think that I'm that sort of woman? For your information, Matteo Moretti, I'm extremely selective when it comes to men! I've been on my own, even though I've had boyfriends, for *years*!'

'And then I come along?' Matteo asked speculatively. 'My mind is beginning to work overtime.'

What could she say to that?

'I didn't foresee...what happened between us.' Rosie suddenly found herself on the back foot.

'Even though you're extremely selective.'

'We were thrown together in a highly charged situation...'

'I was very happy to be the perfect gentleman and sleep on the *chaise longue*, although the ground would have been more comfortable.'

'Yes, well...'

'Let's drop this conversation. It's not going anywhere.'

He reached out, curled his fingers into her unruly, vanilla-blonde hair and tugged her gently towards him.

With helpless fascination, she watched as his mouth descended, and she closed her eyes and whimpered as his cool lips met hers. She curled her fingers onto the waistband of his trousers and felt herself slowly being propelled backwards, ever so slightly, until she bumped against the table behind her.

They were in a public place. A room that was only vacant temporarily because everyone happened to be outside, where the Christmas choir would be starting shortly. What on earth was she doing?

But right now, right here, he *owned* her body and what he was doing with it was turning her on so much she was melting from the inside out. He was kissing her, his tongue lashing against hers…cupping her bottom, massaging it with his big hands…pressing against her so that she could feel the rock-hardness of his erection bulging against his zipper.

Neither heard the door opening behind them. Rosie was certainly oblivious to everything until she heard her mother's shocked voice and then Candice laughing with genuine delight. At which point, she shoved Matteo away. When she looked at her parents—at her entire assembled family, because Emily was there as well—she just wanted the ground to open and swallow her up.

'What are you doing here?' She gasped. 'You're not supposed to be here for another couple of days.'

'Surprise, surprise!' Candice trilled. 'We couldn't wait to come over as soon as we could, and thank goodness that beastly virus was over sooner than expected! We just had time to dump our stuff at the chalet and here we are! Harry spotted the pair of you vanishing into this room so we thought we'd give you a happy surprise!'

Happy surprise? Rosie thought in horror. Of all the adjectives she could come up with, *happy* wasn't one of them. And whatever happened to that old-fashioned courtesy of knocking?

She cleared her throat but her father was already striding towards Matteo, and Rosie could tell from the expression on his face that he wasn't going to oh-so-politely pretend that he hadn't seen them a hair's breadth away from doing more than just a bit of kissing and groping.

She was hot with mortification. She'd always been a daddy's girl and she hated the thought of him being shocked at what he would consider inappropriate behaviour, given the surroundings. They were in a resort in which they'd all been well known as regulars for many years.

'Dad…'

'So you're the young man Candice has told us about!'

'We were just about to go back outside,' Rosie said weakly. 'Great that you're all over!

Hi, Em. Is everyone here? The kids and Lucien and Robert as well?' Her voice was letting her down badly, but that was only to be expected, given the nightmarish turn of events.

'Rosie, I'd like to have a word with your young man on his own.'

'Dad...' She cast a panicked sideways glance at Matteo who, after looking momentarily disconcerted, had somehow managed to gather his composure while hers was still all over the place.

Her tall, beautiful mother, so much alike to her two eldest daughters, had opened her arms for a hug and Rosie walked towards her even though her heart had plummeted. Her dad could be ferocious when the mood took him, and especially so when it came to his daughters.

'Ken...' Debbie Carter said in a warning voice, halting him in his tracks. 'I'm sure Rosie's young man would like to relax before the cross examination begins.'

'Besides.' Emily was joining the family circle. 'Lucien and the kids are waiting outside with Robert.'

Rosie stifled a groan of utter despair.

But, Matteo, she noted with grudging admiration and relief, seemed to have everything under control, making suitably polite noises, clearly unfazed that they had been caught in the middle of a groping session worthy of a couple of horny teenagers.

'Just one question, young man,' her father eventually boomed. Whatever Matteo had been saying, she hadn't clocked all of it, because her mother had been chattering away a mile a minute about this and that. 'I've looked you up on the Internet, although I've heard your name before.'

'Of course.' Matteo accepted the recognition with a sweeping lack of false modesty.

'You're rich,' Ken tabulated on his fingers, 'You have a history of going out with beautiful, high-flying women and yet here you are with my baby.'

'Dad!' Rosie couldn't have got any redder but her father paid absolutely no notice to her horrified interruption.

'I don't take kindly to anyone dabbling with any of my daughters.'

'Don't blame you,' Matteo returned equably, giving Ken Carter as good as he got without any show of disrespect. He certainly wasn't in the least intimidated by the older man. 'If I had a daughter, I would certainly not want anyone fooling around with her feelings.'

'I *am* here!' Rosie interjected in a high

voice, breaking free from her mother and moving to stand between the two men.

They couldn't have been more different physically. Matteo, tall and so dramatically good-looking. Her father, short and rotund, but with the sort of fiercely determined face that advertised why he had managed to get as far as he had.

'My intentions towards your daughter are entirely honourable.'

'Are they?' Ken growled.

'Honourable enough to ensure an engagement ring will soon be on her finger.'

The silence that greeted this statement was so complete that they could have heard a pin drop.

Then screeches of delight came from her sisters, who rushed towards her, warm pleasure from her mother, who was trying to get a word in edgeways, and a grunt of approval from her dad, now shaking Matteo's hand vigorously, warmly, clapping him on the back and announcing that a weight had been lifted from his shoulders.

'She's my little baby,' Rosie was aware of him saying, while sick perspiration began rising from her toes upwards. 'Needs someone to look after her. Glad she's found that person.'

In a daze, Rosie was vaguely aware of her

family all leaving the room *en masse*. Lucien and Robert had apparently chosen to stay outside with the kids, who were in seventh heaven, because Santa was due to make an appearance.

In her elf outfit, and shorn of all festive spirit, all Rosie could think was, *what the heck has just happened...?*

CHAPTER EIGHT

THE REMAINDER OF the evening passed in a blur. Rosie mingled with all the guests, entertaining the kids as Santa's jolly helper while frantically trying to keep her eye on a roaming Matteo. Roaming where and doing what? She wished she had eyes on the back of her head and consoled herself with the thought that he couldn't do any more damage than he had already done.

Engaged? Diamonds on fingers? What on earth had he been thinking?

She fumed internally, because a complicated situation had suddenly got a whole lot more complicated, and yet...

Something inside her burned with treacherous heat at the thought of being engaged to Matteo, wearing his ring on her finger, looking forward to a lifetime of making love with him and finding out more and more what made him tick.

From the very moment he'd entered her life, a curiosity had been awakened inside her that she knew, realistically, would never be sated. Whatever mess he had landed them both in, whatever *further* mess—she had started the ball rolling with her little white lie—this was and never would be a real relationship, one in which sharing and confiding played a part, in which discovery was part of the package.

She was one of the last to leave, because the staff were asked to volunteer for tidying up duties, and it was after eight by the time everything was more or less in order and normality had been restored.

She was standing uncertainly by the Christmas tree in the foyer, fiddling with her hat and wondering how her overwhelming family could be swamping her one minute and nowhere to be seen the next, when a dark, amused and familiar voice said from behind, 'The elf looks somewhat worse for wear.'

Rosie spun round, heart picking up pace and body racing into fifth gear at the sight of him. *He* certainly didn't look the worse for wear. If anything, an evening spent immersed in the Christmas spirit appeared to have relaxed him, although he was so clever at projecting a public face that she wasn't sure whether this was accurate or not.

He'd shoved up the sleeves of his shirt and her eyes were helplessly drawn to his powerful forearms, liberally sprinkled with dark hair. Her mouth went dry and for a few seconds she forgot that she was fuming and angry with him, and had been all evening for the extravagant lie he had told.

'Where's...everyone?' she asked.

'Gone to a French restaurant for dinner. *En masse*.'

'They didn't tell me that that was the plan.'

'That's because I assured them that we would be far keener to break bread together, just the two of us.'

'You're right.' Rosie was proud of her composure as she began walking towards the cloakroom so that she could retrieve her coat, bag and everything else. 'We need to talk.' She felt a lot less jumpy saying this with her back to him. The second he was staring at her with those amazing eyes, her thoughts began going haywire and she couldn't seem to string a coherent sentence together.

She disappeared into the cloakroom and emerged back in sensible clothing but feeling just as dishevelled.

'Let's get something to eat,' Matteo drawled, lounging against the wall with one finger hooked into the waistband of his trousers. 'Long, meaningful conversations are always more productive over food. Where do you want to go?'

Rosie couldn't think of doing anything as relaxing as eating when her mind was buzzing with all sorts of angry, confused thoughts, but she was ravenous. There had been a lot on offer in terms of canapés, but those had been out of bounds to the staff, and she had been too wired to eat any of the leftovers once the tidying had been done. Her stomach growled.

'I'm not actually hungry,' she returned coolly.

'Let's go to the restaurant here. The food is decent enough, from what I recall. And, before you start trying to convince me that you couldn't eat a thing, your stomach has just given you away. You're right, we have to talk, and I won't be doing that standing here outside the cloakroom.'

He pushed himself away from the wall and looked down at her and while she was dithering, loath to give in to his calmly spoken statement of fact, he spun round on his heels and began heading towards the flight of stairs that swept up to the restaurant on the mezzanine floor.

Gritting her teeth with frustration, Rosie pelted behind him, caught up with him. She had a moment of feeling utterly awkward when they were shown to a corner table in the restaurant because, although the coat, scarf and long, black cardigan were all in place, underneath was the elf outfit which wasn't exactly appropriate wear for a serious conversation.

However, there was nothing to be done about that, and she reluctantly surrendered the coat and long, winding scarf to the *maître d'*, making sure to keep the cardigan tightly pulled around her as she took her seat.

Her breasts felt huge, pushing against the stretchy outfit. She had removed the jaunty hat but her fair hair was all over the place and she ran her fingers through it now, trying to get it into some kind of order, her blue eyes very firmly fastened to Matteo's dark, lean face.

'I can see that you can't wait to tell me what's on your mind.' He lounged back in the chair, summoning the waiter over with the smallest of nods and ordering a bottle of Chablis without bothering to look at either the waiter or the wine list, instead keeping his gaze very firmly pinned to her flushed face.

'Can you blame me? How could you?'

'Why don't you take the cardigan off? You must be hot.'

'Thanks for the concern, Matteo, but I'm just fine. And you haven't answered my question—how could you tell my parents, *my whole family,* that we're going to get engaged? How could you pretend that this is actually a serious relationship!' Tears of frustration sprang to her eyes and she rapidly blinked them away.

The waiter came and poured the wine and she muttered what she wanted to eat—the first thing she spotted on the menu that she liked, knowing that she wouldn't do justice to the food that would be placed in front of her.

Matteo leaned towards her, his voice low and cool. 'When I met your sister, I got an idea of how your family operated. She flew down to attack me out of nowhere because she mistakenly thought that I had led you on and broken up with you. She was as ferocious as a tiger looking out for her cub. When you told me that you had lied about being involved with me in order to get out of an uncomfortable Christmas spent with your family trying to match-make you with some guy you weren't interested in, well, needless to say I had never come across a situation like that in my life before.'

Rosie reddened, knowing just how that

made her sound—feeble, childish and not in control of her own life.

'We've been over all of this before,' she muttered with simmering resentment. 'It still doesn't explain why you said what you said.'

'Rosie.' He raked his fingers through his hair and sat back, sipping some of the wine and looking at her carefully, as though doing his best to marshal his thoughts. 'Your sister was just the tip of the iceberg. You are surrounded by family who clearly feel it's their duty to protect you.'

'It's not that unusual.' She squirmed and when she met his eyes his expression was remote.

'In my world, it's very unusual.'

With a tug of compassion, Rosie reached out, but he didn't take her hand and she withdrew it and returned it to her lap.

Of course, he wouldn't understand her family dynamics, she thought, ashamed because she had thoughtlessly put her foot in it. Again.

'I'm sorry, Matteo…'

Matteo held up his hand impatiently to cut short her stammered, sympathetic interruption. 'No need to be. I'm getting accustomed to your outbursts of sympathy. It's irrelevant. The fact is that your father, in particular, is extremely protective of you. I'm guessing that's because you're the baby of the family.'

Rosie shrugged and lowered her eyes. 'We have a lot of shared interests,' she admitted. 'My sisters have never been interested in sport and I was always the one he took to football matches. He used to tell me that it was the best relaxation he could think of after slaving away in an office five days a week.'

He, more than her mother, had been the one to indulge her nomadic lifestyle, she was now forced to concede. Her mother had made lots of noises over the years about her settling down, but her dad had always been the one to overrule those small protests.

Now, she wondered whether it hadn't been partly because her father, born into privilege, had had his life conditioned from an early age. He had been sent to the right schools and gone to the right university and maybe there had been a part of him that had always longed to rebel. Just a little. And that part had led life vicariously through his youngest daughter who had always been a free spirit.

Perhaps that was why, when Bertie had been presented as a possible suitor—her dad had climbed on board that wagon with the rest of the family—it had panicked her because everything had suddenly seemed very serious. A serious, suitable candidate to rescue her from her enjoyable but essentially irresponsible life.

If she hadn't been so panicked, she would never have done what she had done—told that little white lie, never realising what the consequences might be.

'He was never really worried by all those dalliances you had in the past, was he, *cara*? Your father?'

'What makes you say that?' She lifted startled eyes to his and frowned.

'It was a conclusion I reached off my own bat,' Matteo admitted. 'And he said as much to me when I had a conversation earlier on with him.'

'What?' She stared at him furiously and he stared right back at her without blinking an eye. 'What were you doing talking to my dad?'

'Don't be disingenuous, Rosie.'

'What did he say?'

'Exactly that. You deserved to have some fun. You were never academic like your sisters, and if you wanted to stretch your wings a little then he could more than afford to indulge you. But he finally reached the conclusion that it was time for you to discover the joys of leading a more grounded existence, so to speak.'

'You had no right to discuss me behind my back!' she snapped, her voice steeped with dismay. 'And I'm not just a carefree twenty-something!'

'Aren't you?' Matteo questioned and that hurt. For a short while, she couldn't speak at all, and it was a relief that their starters were being positioned in front of them, small, tasty dishes, because it relieved her of the need to say anything.

'You think I don't find that an attractive trait?' he asked gruffly, and her eyes shot to his face.

'What are you talking about?'

'You're like a breath of fresh air and I think I may have mentioned that to you before,' Matteo admitted with rough sincerity. 'I've never met anyone like you in my life before.'

'What does that have to do with…anything? Matteo, it would have been so much easier if you hadn't said what you had. Relationships come and go, and if this one crashed and burned, then…'

'Then it would have joined all the rest of your relationships that had crashed and burned in the past?'

Rosie gazed at him with down-turned mouth.

'Why should you care?' Her voice was so low that Matteo had to strain forward to hear what she had said.

Good point, he thought uncomfortably. There was no reason why he *should* care. He just knew that what he had seen in her during the short time he had known her had fired up in him something strangely protective. Her entire family had descended and when her father had cornered him he had reacted utterly on impulse. For once in his life, Matteo had been galvanised into behaviour that was alien to him.

The only thought that had run through his head was, *they know who I am and they're already predicting the outcome. Another failed relationship, and this time one deserving of even more tea and sympathy because of who I am.*

Underneath the sunny, plucky exterior was someone both sensitive and oddly brave. She needed to find her place in the family dynamics and suddenly he had been driven by the urge to help her along.

Matteo wasn't going to delve further into his motivations. Introspection never got anyone anywhere because, when it came to the crunch, action and not thought was what mattered.

But tugging away at the back of his mind was the notion that perhaps not everyone fought the same battles he had. It wasn't always about carving out a place for yourself in the world of money. Sometimes, there were other forces at work. It didn't mean that the fight was any the less significant.

He shrugged. 'Maybe I didn't care for either the idea that I would be just the sort to take advantage of an innocent like you, because of the person I'm reported as being in the media, or the idea that you would be disingenuous enough to walk straight into a trap from which you could only end up hurt, requiring your over-protective family to go into rallying mode.'

'So you decided to become the knight in shining armour?'

'That wasn't the intention but I'm happy to go along with the description.'

'Except,' she said ruefully, 'That still leaves us the problem of breaking up from a so-called serious relationship where we're about to get engaged.'

'No,' Matteo corrected, 'That leaves *you* walking away from a serious relationship where we're about to get engaged. That puts *you* firmly in the role of heartbreaker.' He grinned. 'I have a feeling that if you play your cards right your family will have a lot of respect for your decision.'

'Why would you do that for me?'

'Maybe I think you're worth it.'

Rosie nodded with a thoughtful frown but inside her nerves were all over the place.

What did it mean?

They had been thrown together because of her rash outburst and she had assumed, from day one, that they were so dissimilar that, even having slept together, there was no way he could ever find her interesting. Not really.

And vice versa, naturally.

But a tiny voice now asked…did they actually have what it took to have a relationship? A proper relationship?

A curious thrill rippled through her, the thrill of the great, big unknown, of an adventure waiting to happen.

'Yes.' She unconsciously glanced at her finger and wondered what a diamond ring would look like on it, then she closed her hand into a fist and banished the thought, because this wasn't real. There would be no genuine 'for ever after' relationship. He'd felt sorry for her. Underneath the tough exterior, she couldn't have found a nicer guy even though she didn't think he'd thank her if she pointed that out.

'You have no idea what kind of Pandora's box you've opened,' was what she said instead. 'My parents aren't going to be casual about this. My mum will already be planning what outfit she'll be wearing, and whether it would be too premature to have a chat with the local vicar, and they'll both be debating whether they should have a marquee on the lawn like they did for both my sisters.'

She closed her eyes and contemplated the dreadful scenario unfolding in front of her. 'But you're right. You're such a catch, they'll respect me for turning down your proposal.' She smiled, a wide, sunny smile. 'A passing fling, well, they would have been sympathetic, but a full-blown marriage proposal— I'm not sure if they'll know quite how to react.'

'You're fortunate,' he said in a husky undertone and Rosie glanced up at him in bewilderment. 'You have people who care deeply about you.'

'They care so much that they don't understand that there were times when I felt stifled,' Rosie said bluntly. She felt as though something inside her had toughened up. The girl who had rushed into a little white lie to spare herself the annoyance of Bertie, his nerdy persistence and irritating habits was gone for ever. In its place was someone slowly realising that she needed to be in charge of her future, stronger, more assured, more focused.

'There were times when *I* didn't realise just how stifled I felt.'

'So you took to the hills and ran as fast as you could?'

Rosie laughed, marvelling that he could be so perceptive. 'They were always terribly understanding about my academic failures.'

'Maybe they shouldn't have been,' Matteo said mildly. He reached forward absently to graze her knuckles with his thumb.

'We're having a deep and meaningful conversation,' Rosie remarked and then wished she hadn't because he immediately withdrew his hand with a frown.

'We're discussing a way forward with this,' he responded quickly. 'I took this charade past the bedroom door and into the bed.'

'You slept on the sofa,' Rosie was quick to remind him. She wanted him to reach out and take her hand again. She missed the warmth, the feel of his finger casually stroking her bare skin. 'And you would have carried on sleeping there until your deal got signed and you were free to leave.'

'I opened the Pandora's box,' Matteo said drily. 'But let's forget about who did what. We weren't having a deep and meaningful conversation. We were discussing what happens next and how best to deal with the fallout.'

He shifted, uneasy and suddenly restless.

The logic of his argument was reassuring. 'Let's face it, Rosie—when I walk away from this, I won't have any further contact with you or your family. You will be the one left to handle the inevitable post mortem. It's to your advantage if you're given a helping hand in tackling the aftermath.'

'Of course.' She linked her fingers together and stared at them. That told her, she thought, just in case she started getting any ideas. She doubted he even realised the subliminal warning. 'What if word gets out?'

'What do you mean?'

'Social media is everywhere. People with mobile phones taking pictures. What if someone you work with finds out that you somehow got yourself engaged while you were over here on business? And then got cruelly dumped?'

Matteo grinned. 'I like the way you're going to cruelly dump me. I'd bet that there might be a few women out there who would enjoy hearing that.' He became more sober. 'Go ahead and be as heartless as you like. I don't care what other people think of me.'

Somewhere along the line, food had been eaten and wine had been drunk. Matteo hadn't really noticed. He had been way too absorbed in the woman sitting opposite him, absorbed to the exclusion of everything else, and that in itself was a source of wonder because he couldn't recall the last time any woman had commanded that sort of attention from him.

Work absorbed him. Women relaxed him. Not this one. His life had been a rollercoaster ride since meeting her and it surprised him to acknowledge that, as hair-raising experiences went, this one was pretty exhilarating.

He watched her with brooding intent, his keen eyes noting everything about her softly appealing face, from the delicate tinge of colour staining her cheeks to the glittering blue of her eyes and the fullness of her parted mouth. Then he thought of her in bed, naked and eager, her full roundness, her heavy breasts, such a sexy contrast to the angular women who constituted his usual diet. He felt himself harden at the thought of her.

'I envy you not caring what other people

think of you,' she was saying as their eyes tangled. 'If I had half of your indifference, we wouldn't be sitting here right now.'

'But you wouldn't be you if you had half of my indifference and who says that I'm not enjoying myself sitting here right now?'

Her tongue darted out, moistening her upper lip, and Matteo had to stop himself from groaning.

'Stop doing that,' she whispered, lowering her gaze, but almost immediately returning greedy eyes to his lean, handsome face.

'Doing what?'

'Staring at me...like that.'

'Like what?'

'You know.'

'Oh, I know.' He laughed under his breath. 'I just want to hear you say it.'

'You're looking at me as though you could...'

'Eat you?' He raised his eyebrows expressively. 'It's exactly what I want to do, *mia cara*. I want to feast on your body, suckle your breasts until you're squirming underneath me, and then I want to take you until you cry out and beg for me to never stop.'

'Matteo!' She squirmed and looked around her, red-faced.

'Let's get out of here.'

A thought suddenly struck her. 'We should. We can't have the whole troop return to the lodge to find that your things are in the spare room!'

'Don't panic. I removed myself for the night, not for the long haul, and if the bed isn't made quite as it should be then who's to say that we haven't spread ourselves around the house in our uncontrollable need to pleasure one another, irrespective of whether it's your bedroom or not?' He burst out laughing as crimson colour stole into her face. 'Don't look so shocked. It happens.'

He beckoned across a waiter with a crook of his finger and tossed his credit card down without bothering to check the bill. 'I'll enjoy showing you the ropes.'

Rosie had no need to ask what he meant and she blushed furiously, her whole body going up in flames with anticipation and excitement.

'Come on.'

'Where are we going?' she asked, breathless, cardigan still pulled tightly around her as she followed him out of the restaurant. Instead of heading towards the cloakroom so that she could fetch her coat, they headed towards the reception desk where she was greeted like an old friend.

'I think we can spend the night here, don't you?' He slid her a sideways glance.

If he wanted their pretend relationship to hit the gossip grapevine fast, then he couldn't have chosen a more efficient method. They all knew her here at the hotel, and sharing a room with him...?

A flare of adrenaline-charged excitement coursed through her. She felt faint and she had to look away as he sorted out the most expensive suite for them.

'This is crazy. Mum and Dad...everyone... will be expecting us to show up at the chalet after dinner.'

'Mum and Dad and everyone else will be raising their glasses to the wildly enamoured couple. If you're planning on forging a way forward as someone with a voice, then you could start using it right now. Besides, I can't wait, and I don't want to get back to the chalet to find myself bogged down making small talk until midnight.'

'I can't wait, either,' she confessed, as they made their way to the lift, on a heated sigh. Her hand was trembling as she extracted her mobile phone and punched in Candice's number. She sent a text because she didn't know if she would be able to sound controlled should a conversation ensue.

The lift doors opened and as soon as they had whirred shut behind them he pulled her to him. His head descended and his mouth crushed hers hungrily, his tongue plundering her mouth until her legs felt as weak as jelly and she had to cling to him for support, like a rag doll. She pushed her hands underneath his clothes, finding bare, warm skin, and she shoved them up to rub his flat nipples. His body was hard and sinewy. She wanted to explore every inch of it, to feel every corded muscle, sinew and tendon.

In a minute, she thought weakly, the lift doors were going to open and they would be faced with some shocked faces, but they made it to their floor in privacy, and by the time he was unlocking the door to the suite with the gold-and-black card she was desperate to get rid of her clothes.

They stumbled into the huge sitting area, bodies urgently pressed together. He was stripping along the way, blindly leading her in the general direction of the bedroom until he abandoned their stumbling progress and swept her off her feet, kicking open the door.

The bedroom was bathed in the peculiar glow only falling snow outside could cause and he left the curtains open. She was on the mattress of the super-king-sized bed without even realising how she had got there, and she hastily propped herself up on her elbows, watching as he stripped off.

He was so glorious he took her breath away. So glorious that nothing else mattered. Not her family, not what other people might start thinking, not the aftermath of this madness waiting to catch her out.

The only thought in her head was, *I want this guy more than anything.*

The wretched elf outfit had to come off but he stilled her frantic hands as she began to scrabble with buttons, the zip and various bits of Velcro, all of which seemed to be oddly positioned in ridiculously unreachable places.

'I want to see you do a striptease,' he murmured, his voice as dark and as seductive as chocolate. 'I want to enjoy watching you. You have an amazing body.'

He held out his hand, their fingers linked and then she was on her feet and he was on the bed, places reversed. He, utterly naked, and she…

Bit by bit the clothing was removed and bit by languorous bit she began to enjoy herself. Initial nerves were replaced by brazen relish. His eyes on her were such a turn on and she was wet and on fire by the time the last strip of elf costume had been flung to the ground.

She sashayed her way towards him and stood by the side of the bed, and he sat up to slip his hand between her thighs, parting them, feeling the wetness there against his hand. Then he gently parted the delicate folds of her womanhood and flicked his tongue along the groove, finding the stiffened bud of her clitoris with ease.

Rosie moaned and arched back, automatically opening her legs wider to receive his exploring tongue. She moved against him, hands reaching down to press his head harder against her so that he could taste her even more thoroughly.

As he licked, he caressed the soft flesh of her inner thighs, stroking lightly until she was going crazy with desire. She wanted to come against his mouth and yet she never wanted the rolling waves of sensation to end.

He took her so far and then pulled her down to the bed to join him. This time, their love-making was fast, hard and furious and her orgasm was explosive, coming even as she felt him arch back and groan loudly, succumbing to his own release.

She was utterly spent when he eventually positioned her onto her side so that they were facing one another. She looked at him drowsily, smiled and stroked the side of his face.

'We're not in a trap.' Matteo kissed the side of her mouth, the angles of his lean face thrown into shadow because his back was to the window. 'So the charade went a little further than originally intended but is that such a bad thing?'

'What do you mean?'

'I mean this...us.' He swept his hand along her thigh and she shivered. 'This ridiculous chemistry... So, we're chalk and cheese and what we have isn't going to last. You know that and I know that but for now... God, I want you, *tesoro mio*. When I think of you, I want you, and I want you immediately. I touch you and I don't want the touching to end. This charade...why don't we enjoy it for what it is and forget about tomorrow?'

CHAPTER NINE

ROSIE DIDN'T WANT to think it but she did anyway: *this is perfect.*

She and Matteo were standing on an incline, looking down at a Christmas extravaganza. It was a little after seven and the slopes were ablaze with lights. The sound of laughter and kids screeching with excitement were only just drowned out by the harmonious singing of the Christmas choir, who were perched on a makeshift stage just outside one of the five star resorts in radiant reds, whites, *faux* furs and boots.

For the first time in days, the snow had stopped falling, conspiring to provide a picture-postcard image of what the perfect December evening should look like.

Of course, she guiltily acknowledged to herself, the reason it was perfect was because Matteo was standing next to her with one arm carelessly slung round her waist. They were both drinking mulled wine and Rosie was heady with happiness.

She'd never thought that it was possible for her to be quite so happy. Her family adored Matteo. After her father's initial misgivings, they had all succumbed to his charm. He could hold court without seeming to and what she might once have considered the hugely annoying trait, being just so self-assured, she now found deliciously mesmerising.

It was really no wonder her entire family had been sucked into his magic circle. She could only imagine their giddy relief at the fact that she was supposedly engaged to a guy like him, settled with someone of whom they heartily approved.

She didn't want to think about how they would react when it ended. She didn't want to think of all those scary tomorrows and what they might herald. Three days ago, he had dangled that carrot in front of her: enjoy the chemistry they shared and forget about tomorrow. She had grabbed that carrot with both hands. She was going to live for today. She was going to savour the excitement, the wonder of being with an unsuitable guy who still, somehow, managed to make her blood boil hot in her veins. She was going to enjoy losing herself in the glory of his love-making. Beyond that, anything could happen. In theory.

'Miss your family not being here?' Matteo inclined his head to murmur into her ear and Rosie shivered and looked up at him. In the reflected glow from all those thousands of lights that illuminated the snow-covered slopes, his face was all shadows and angles.

She thought about it. 'Normally I would,' she confessed. 'But I'll be seeing them on Christmas Eve when we…er…when I go back to England. It's unusual for me to be here at this time of year. It's because I'm instructing.'

She gulped down some of the mulled wine. Would Matteo be returning to England with her? And would he be spending Christmas with her entire family at her parents' country house in the Cotswolds? Or would he be going his own way, doing his own thing? She didn't want to ask the question because she was afraid that the answer might not be to her liking. The deal with Bob and Margaret had been signed and now there was nothing binding him to her, aside from the chemistry.

In his *let's enjoy this and forget about tomorrow* suggestion he had failed to clarify what counted as 'tomorrow' and she didn't want to press him for an answer.

'Are *you* going to miss them?' she asked teasingly. 'I expect you've found it all a little…chaotic. It always is when we all get together, especially with the kids, and especially at this time of year.'

'It's been an experience.' Matteo shrugged. 'This would not be how I would usually spend the run up to Christmas Day but, as experiences go, I am certainly glad I've had it.'

'That's good,' Rosie said uncertainly. She laughed. 'I think.'

'I'll certainly be glad to have the place to ourselves once again.' Matteo lowered his voice and brushed his lips against her cheek. 'There's something unnerving about making love when outside there's the danger of two little people banging on the bedroom door and demanding interaction in whatever game they've decided to play.'

'They liked you,' Rosie said.

'Don't sound so shocked,' Matteo commented wryly, leading her down towards the lit slopes where the carollers were finishing the last of their repertoire. He still had his arm around her waist and she was leaning into him.

'I bet you never come into contact with anyone under the age of…let me think about this…maybe twenty-one? The average age for new recruits to join a company after university?'

'You forget,' Matteo surprised himself by pointing out, drawing her closer against him, 'That I grew up surrounded by a lot of kids. When I hit twelve, I was given the task of looking after a number of the younger ones.' He laughed at the surprise on her face. 'And don't tell me that you're sorry because you've suddenly remembered my very different childhood.'

'You took care of the other kids?'

'It was company policy, so to speak. You would be surprised at how many of them were off the rails by the time they hit six.'

'You don't like talking about your past.'

'I've never seen the point of dwelling on things that cannot be changed.'

'Have you ever confided in anyone?'

'By anyone, you mean a therapist?' Matteo burst out laughing. 'That touchy-feely stuff isn't for me.'

'There's a lot to be said for that touchy-feely stuff,' Rosie said pensively. She shivered as his hand crept under her thick, padded, heavily insulated jacket to caress a sliver of skin under the waistband of her ski trousers. 'I'm a great believer in sharing…what's on your mind.'

'I know.' Matteo grinned down at her. 'You're excellent at letting me know all the highways and byways of what you're thinking.'

'Do you find it boring?' She stiffened and pulled away from the light caress.

'You'd know about it if I did.'

'How? Would you tell me?' She looked up at him seriously, wishing she could read his face, wishing she had as much insight into the workings of his mind as he obviously thought he had into hers. Wishing that the playing field was a little more level.

'I wouldn't have to.'

The carollers disbanded and normality returned, although skiing was now being replaced by *après ski* and the crowds were dissipating, with clusters of warmly wrapped people hiving off in whatever direction their various resorts, chalets and hotels lay.

The loss of that background carolling suddenly made the cold, wintry slopes feel very quiet, very still. 'I meant have you ever confided in any of your girlfriends in the past?'

'No,' Matteo said abruptly.

Rosie ventured boldly into the unknown. 'You've never felt close enough to anyone to talk to them about your past?'

'I'm trying and failing to see where this conversation is heading.'

'It isn't heading anywhere.' She sighed.

'Good,' he said silkily. 'Now, where do you want to eat? Are you hungry? We could always skip an elaborate meal and head back to the chalet. I'm looking forward to having the place to ourselves.'

'So you've said.' She kept her voice as bright as she could but this time it felt like an effort.

He was looking forward to an empty chalet because without anyone around he could, taking his time and without fear of interruption, do what he did best. Make love. Wonderful, stupendous, fabulous sex. But that was where it ended. He wasn't interested in being alone with her so that they could share anything more significant than their bodies.

Rosie hated herself for letting her thoughts stray into that dangerous territory. She was determined to think and live in the moment but her heart clenched in disappointment and frustration.

'Eat, I think.' She needed a bit of time to get back into the right frame of mind, away from the barrage of muddled thoughts assailing her. 'The café in that resort halfway down the hill is very good. Although it might be packed.'

He *had* confided in her, Rosie thought as they slowly made their way past busy, brightly lit restaurants, cafés and boutiques, past the laughing, chattering crowds. He had told her stuff about his past, but did she occupy a unique position because of that? Or had he said as little as he possibly could simply because, in this game of theirs, he'd decided that she needed, at the very least, to have some sketchy background information about him?

And the information had been delivered without the benefit of emotion. He had simply told her facts about himself without telling her how those facts had impacted on him, made him the person that he had become.

It wasn't his fault that his omissions had left her more curious rather than less.

The café was crowded but a table was miraculously produced for them from thin air. She had noticed that he had that impact on people and it wasn't simply because he oozed wealth. It was a combination of his striking good looks and his cool assumption that the duty of everyone around him was to jump through hoops to give him what he demanded.

That curious blend of urbane sophistication and dangerous, wrong-side-of-the-tracks toughness inspired awe, fascination and a healthy respect in everyone he met.

She couldn't imagine what it might be like to work for him. He had offered her a job in one of his companies as a way to becoming independent once they returned to London but she had immediately turned him down. It had felt like a salve to his conscience for any discomfort he might subconsciously feel when their time was up. But, when she thought about him no longer being in her life at all, she felt sick. He had made her question her life and her choices and that had been a good thing, long overdue, but had his offer been genuine? It would certainly be useful, at least to start, if she were to enter the work force as opposed to returning to full-time education, which was also an option.

And she might get to see him. He wouldn't vanish completely out of her life. He would still be *there*. Maybe, subconsciously, by offering her a job, he had been thinking the same thing…?

All those questions were finding air time in her head as she sat down so it was hardly surprising that the woman's voice from behind her took a while to penetrate.

She wasn't expecting it. She wasn't expecting anyone to recognise Matteo and she spun around as he stood up, his silver-grey eyes revealing nothing, although he was smiling at the tall, striking brunette weaving her way towards them.

Rosie watched.

An old flame. That was the thought that raced through her head. The woman was in her thirties, with a sharp, dark bob. She was very tall, very slender and very pale.

'Bethany.' Matteo made the introductions, his voice formal and polite. 'This is… Rosie.'

'Rosie…' Bethany's curious brown eyes looked at Rosie, gauging, intelligent, speculative. 'Have we met anywhere? I don't believe I recognise you. Are you and Matteo…?'

'Tell me what you're doing here, Bethany. Didn't think you found much time to take to the slopes. Join us for a drink?'

'Quick Chablis? Rob's going to be joining me in twenty minutes. You remember Rob, don't you? Melstorm? Head of Asset Management at Frazier and Co? We're an item now.' She flashed an enormous engagement ring in their general direction and sat at the chair Matteo had pulled out for her.

At which point, Rosie was relegated to spectator.

It wasn't so much an intimate catch-up as a conversation about finance and what was going on in their relative worlds of law, asset management, mergers and acquisitions and big business. Names were bandied about and small in-jokes made that elicited the sort of secret smiles from the brunette that made Rosie's teeth snap together.

Chablis finished and about to leave, Bethany finally turned her attention to Rosie and asked pleasantly what she did for a living.

'Don't tell me,' she drawled lightly, head tilted to one side as though trying to work out a conundrum, convinced that the right answer would be found. 'Maybe company lawyer for one of those start-up companies? Dylan Sync, maybe? If this rogue's dating you—and I gather he must be, because it's not exactly his thing to be in the company of any woman he isn't dating unless he's in an office wearing a suit—then you surely must be big in the corporate world.'

Rosie stiffened, sensing an attack under the glossy smile.

'I must be the exception to the rule because I... I'm currently employed as a ski instructor at the resort a little further up the slopes.'

'You're a *ski instructor*?' Bethany stared at her as though she had suddenly grown two heads and then she burst out laughing. 'I don't believe it!' She waggled her fingers in a little wave at the fiancé who was obviously behind them 'Matteo Moretti and a ski instructor! That's a first. You must have something special, my dear!'

'I suppose I must have.' Rosie realised in that instant that Matteo wasn't going to intervene, he wasn't going to stand up for her, and that hurt because it put everything in perspective. 'What do you think, Matteo?'

'I think it's getting late and it's probably time we headed back to the lodge.'

'How did you two meet? I'm curious.' Bethany's eyes darted slyly between the two of them.

'How we met is irrelevant,' Matteo drawled. 'Good luck with the wedding, Bethany. Should I expect an invite to land on my doormat in due course?'

'Oh, I shouldn't think so, Matteo.' Her brown eyes cooled. 'I don't think Rob would like that very much. Ex-heartbreakers always pose a threat.'

Then she laughed again and said to Rosie, 'Have fun with Matteo, Little Miss Ski Instructor, but be warned—he's not a guy who likes sticking around for any length of time!'

'Don't worry about me.' Rosie bared her

teeth in a stiff smile. 'I won't be leaving this with a broken heart.' She saw, from Bethany's face, that her jibe had hit home. It wasn't in her nature to be uncharitable, but this time it felt pretty good.

Little Miss Ski Instructor? No way was she going to get away with that dismissive insult.

But this was the sort of woman Matteo enjoyed and not just for her novelty value. This was the sort of woman who appealed to him on an intellectual front. Rosie had watched the way they had talked to one another, their conversation on a level she could barely keep up with. They had friends in common, work in common—an interest in the business of making money in common.

'Apologies,' Matteo said, turning to her.

'Why?'

'You were uncomfortable. I had no idea Bethany would be here.'

'If you thought that I was uncomfortable, then why didn't you say something?'

'Say something?'

'I get it that she was an ex-flame, and you had lots of exciting catching up to do about the stock market and which dull company was doing what, but it got personal, Matteo.' Rosie's heart was thudding so hard, it was making her giddy. 'She was just plain nasty to me and the least you could have done was to say something. When did you two break up anyway?'

Matteo looked at her narrowly and in silence. 'Where are you going with all this?'

'I'm not *going* anywhere. I'm reacting just the way any other woman you were sleeping with would react!'

Pinned to the wall, Matteo experienced a surge of searing discomfort. She never backed down. He should know that trait of hers by now. She was persistent with him in a way no one else was. She didn't wince or back away in the face of his obvious, unflinching disapproval. He didn't want to discuss Bethany, or any of his ex-girlfriends, for that matter. She should be able to suss that out. He knew that she did, but she just kept crashing through his boundary lines as though they didn't exist.

What was it with the woman? Did he need this?

'How would *you* feel if some ex-flame of mine showed up and was rude to you? How would *you* feel if I just stood there and didn't say anything?'

'I wouldn't have a hysterical outburst,' Matteo returned grimly. 'I also wouldn't expect you to rush to my defence.'

'Well, you might have rushed to mine!'

They stared at one another in silence and Rosie was the first to look away. She was feeling so many things. Hurt, disappointment and most of all the sinking knowledge that he felt nowhere near for her what she felt for him. She'd let herself get carried away, had let her imagination play tricks on her, and she was paying the price now. He wasn't going to defend her because he didn't see the point.

'You did a pretty good job of taking Bethany down a peg or two.' Matteo shifted, deeply uncomfortable with the raw emotion of this conversation, yet seemingly unable to shut it down the way he knew he had to.

What was she looking for? He was no one's knight in shining armour. He'd never applied for that job and he never would, and he knew that she deserved better than someone whose entire life had geared him towards turning away from rescuing damsels. But something twisted inside him at the expression on her face.

'You're right. I did.' She paused and looked him in the eye. 'Would you have told her that I was your girlfriend, Matteo? If she hadn't jumped to the conclusion off her own bat? Or would you have passed me off as the ski instructor you were having a drink with because you'd just had a good lesson and wanted to say thank you?'

'Don't be ridiculous,' he said, flushing darkly. 'Why is that women can fixate on one small thing and magnify it to ridiculous proportions?'

'It's patronising to stereotype women and to try and diminish what I'm trying to say. I'm not fixating on *one small thing*. I'm being perfectly reasonable.'

'I can't believe I'm having this conversation.'

'You mean you don't *want* to believe that you are, because the only talking you're interested in doing is between the sheets.'

'It works, doesn't it?' he grated, crashing into the barrier of her arctic coldness and not knowing how to deal with it, because he had become so accustomed to her soft, sweet accommodating nature. She was so ultra-feminine. He angrily wanted to backtrack and rush to her defence, as she'd wanted, just so that he could have her back.

But maybe this was for the best. In fact, it *was* for the best. This was supposed to be fun. He wasn't interested in having to justify his behaviour to anyone. He'd never done that in his life before and he wasn't going to start now.

'You might think it's terrific being repressed,' Rosie said through gritted teeth, getting angrier and angrier by the second, 'But it's not. It's just sad and I feel sorry for you. And, if you don't want to be having this conversation, then that's fine. I'll head back to the chalet and you can do whatever you want. Stay here at the hotel. You've signed your precious deal so there's really no reason for us to carry on with this any more.'

She didn't rush or run off, and anyone might have thought that she was simply getting up to go to the bathroom, but she wasn't looking at him as she weaved her way towards the door, heading straight for the cloakroom so that she could collect her padded jacket.

Would he follow her? Rosie didn't know and she didn't care. She knew that he didn't *do* so many things, of which emotion was obviously one, but his indifference to her feelings hurt her beyond belief.

She thought of Bethany and she felt a rush of pure misery. It was one thing knowing that he went for women like that but it was another thing actually to be confronted by one of them.

That unexpected meeting had really brought home to her that to Matteo this really was just a game and she was no more than a passing indulgence.

Whilst for her...

She couldn't be casual about him the way he was about her because she had made a crucial mistake in her dealings with him. She had somehow managed to pretend that she could be as tough as he was. She had forgotten that she had a heart, and that hearts got broken, and hers was breaking now because she knew, without a shadow of a doubt, that she had stupidly gone and fallen in love with the man.

From pointing at a random stranger in the foyer of the resort, a stranger clearly removed from the festive chaos all around him, she had galloped towards heartbreak. He had seduced her with his wit, his charm, his intelligence and with those glimpses of someone he was at pains to conceal. He had thrown her tantalising titbits about himself and about his childhood and she had gobbled them up and wanted more. What had started as a charade because he wanted to complete a deal, and he needed to go along with the pretence of a relationship with her in order to get there, for her had become an obsession.

And now they were lovers and everything was...*a mess.*

She knew that he was behind her before he said, in a low, gritty voice, 'You don't get to make outrageous statements like the one you just made and then run away.'

'Go away. I don't want to talk to you.'

'Tough. You opened a box and now you don't get to shut the lid until we've gone through all the contents.'

Rosie felt the chill of an imminent break-up whisper over her. Pride came to her defence.

'You're right.' Somehow, they were outside the hotel and heading towards the car. Her feet had propelled her in the right direction and she hadn't even noticed. She wasn't looking at him as she headed to the car and she was revving the engine before she deigned to glance in his direction, and then only briefly. ' I thought that I could do this. I thought I could have a fun fling with you, but you're a stranger, and having a fun fling with a stranger doesn't make me feel good about myself.'

'Where is this coming from? One crazy encounter with an ex?' He frustratedly raked his fingers through his hair.

'It's not about your ex, Matteo. It's about the fact that I don't know you. You keep everything to yourself.'

'You know more about me than any other woman I've ever gone out with.'

And that was why she had deluded herself into thinking that what they had was somehow special. He'd opened up about his past and she had read all sorts of things into that. She'd been wrong to do so.

'Because, as you pointed out,' she said coldly, 'You had no option because of the situation. You were desperate to get your deal done. You had to pretend to be my boyfriend and so you ended up having to share a few details about your past to keep the fiction believable.'

She laughed shortly. 'You couldn't take any chances that Bob and Margaret or someone from my family might ask a question, only to find out that I didn't know a thing about you aside from your name. You shared what you did because you didn't think you had a choice. I don't even know what your deal was all about or why it was so important to you! You never shared *that,* did you?'

'Want to know about the deal, Rosie?'

'Nope. You can carry on being as secretive as you like, Matteo.'

She wasn't going to beg. She'd made the biggest mistake of her life falling in love with him and she only had herself to blame because he had been honest from the start about his intentions: sex, fun and nothing else. She'd chosen to ignore the hand in front of her because trying to rearrange the cards into a different, more exciting hand had been too tempting to resist. In the end, it was always going to come back to the same place, though. They were never going to have a relationship, not the sort of relationship she craved.

It was going to end but she wasn't going to cry, plead or declare her undying love.

They were back at the lodge. She'd barely noticed the short drive. Now, she flipped open the door and jumped out, landing squarely on pristine white, then she trudged to the front door and opened it to let herself in without bothering to look back at him.

'Jesus, Rosie…' He pulled her towards him as she was striding off towards the kitchen. 'The deal…' He shook his head and scowled. 'They own a farm.'

'You don't have to share, Matteo. I told you that.'

'It's no state secret.'

'Then why act like it was?'

'It's who I am.'

Rosie didn't think much of that answer and her expression said as much.

'They're very particular about…the plot of

land that this farm sits on. The land is valuable. It wouldn't be impossible for a developer to get planning permission to stick up a load of executive houses with manicured lawns and double garages. It's in a prime location in the north of England.'

Rosie opened her mouth to repeat that he could keep his story to himself, because it was too late, but curiosity got the better of her.

'Why would making more money by developing land matter so much to you, Matteo? Haven't you got enough?' She wished that she could pigeon-hole him as a greedy capitalist but it didn't work. He had got under her skin by being complicated.

'There's a…for want of a better word… facility there that provides…' He shook his head and stared at her in silence for a few seconds.

'A facility?' Rosie prompted coldly. Was this his idea of a concession? He didn't want to explain his past to her. He had brushed their relationship aside, when put to the test, because for him it didn't actually qualify as a relationship. She had asked him about the deal but did she really care about it? She had cited it because it had been the first example to come to mind of something else he felt compelled to keep silent about. It would be just something else to do with making lots of money. As if he didn't already have enough. He wasn't interested in talking about what she wanted to talk about, which was his emotional past. *That* was very firmly off-limits!

'Maybe *facility* is the wrong word,' Matteo said brusquely, heading for the kitchen. She followed him, marvelling at how he somehow managed to convey the impression that he was master of all he surveyed, even though he was a visitor in her parents' chalet.

He was firing up the coffee machine, his back to her, and there was tension in his posture. When he finally looked at her, his lean, beautiful face was closed.

'Bob and Margaret,' he said quietly, 'have a place on the grounds that provides a working holiday for...the kind of kid I used to be.'

Rosie's heart skipped a beat and she stared at him.

'It's partly educational, with facilities for learning various crafts, but there's also a football field, tennis courts and horse riding on tap. The quality of the buyer is very important to them because they don't want those facilities to be scrapped. There is an enormous amount of acreage and, whilst they concede that some might be developed, they insist as part of the deal that the main place for foster kids remain intact. Naturally, it wouldn't be a legally binding situation. More of a gentleman's agreement.'

'And gentlemen don't lead young girls up the garden path, play with their feelings and then dump them without further ado. You could have told them the truth, which was that you had no idea who I was.'

Matteo shrugged. 'Why waste time on laborious explanations that would still have probably left a sour aftertaste in their mouths when another, far less onerous solution presented itself?'

'You intend to...develop some of the land?' She was enthralled by what he was saying, sliding deeper into love with him, as helpless against her own emotions as a piece of driftwood blown across stormy seas.

'I intend to develop quite a bit of the land,' Matteo told her. 'I intend to expand on the facilities there so that more underprivileged kids can come and stay there and see that there's life beyond the bleak walls of whatever foster care situation they're struggling with. I will ensure that the best of professionals are at hand for educational purposes. I will make it the sort of place... I would have benefited even more from as a youngster. So there you have it, Rosie. Has it lived up to the hype?'

'Why did you tell me?' she asked quietly.

Because I love you, was what she hoped he would say.

'Because you deserve to know,' Matteo told her roughly. And that was as far as he was prepared to go.

His wintry-grey eyes collided with hers and just for a moment…just for a second… something stirred inside him, one of those confusing, inexplicable, seismic shifts that only seemed to happen in her company, a strange feeling of disorientation that defied common sense.

He gritted his teeth together, despising himself for that fleeting loss of self-control.

The truth was that this crazy charade had not panned out the way he had foreseen.

It should have been easy, controllable. He never allowed himself to enter into situations he couldn't control. It was too much like opening the door to a room without knowing what was happening behind it, and there had been way too many of those doors in his childhood.

A sheen of prickly perspiration broke out over his body and he scowled.

Memories. Who needed them? He'd done a

great job of banking down on them over the years, locking them away, always moving onwards and upwards, refusing to be dragged back to a past that was no longer relevant.

Had they begun to wriggle free when he had started dealings with Bob and Margaret?

The land with the care facilities on it—had that kick-started a trip back in time which seemed to have picked up pace just recently?

Or had the woman in front of him somehow opened that door, letting them flood out?

And, if that was the case, how the heck had it happened? Matteo wasn't going to stick around analysing the situation.

'I deserved to know?' Rosie questioned.

'We were where we were because I wanted that land. It's only fair, in the end, that you know the reason why it meant so much to me.'

And no one could accuse Matteo of not being fair, she thought bitterly. He'd been the perfect gentleman who'd kept his distance, and slept on a bed of nails in her bedroom because she'd asked him to, and thereby had opened the first crack in her heart. And he'd been as fair as anyone could be when he'd warned her that he 'didn't do love'. Or sharing. Or jealousy. Or confiding. Or Christmas. He certainly hadn't led her up the garden path with phoney promises about a future that was never going to happen!

And he was being fair now. Giving her the explanation she'd asked for, digging a deeper hole into her heart and showing her just how complex a man he was.

He'd been a gentleman, and he'd been fair and honest, and now it was over because she wanted much more than a fair and honest gentleman. She wanted the whole package, but she was never going to get it, and she couldn't pretend that sleeping with him for a bit longer, until he got bored of her, was better than nothing, because it wasn't.

'Thank you for that,' she said with a stiff smile and keeping her distance. 'I'm glad you told me. I would always have been curious. I've enjoyed being with you Matteo. It was all so unexpected…the turn of events…but I've grown up. I partly have you to thank for that but I can't carry on making love to you until we both get bored. I feel like I'm facing a new chapter in my life and I want to get on with it.'

This was exactly as it should be, Matteo thought. So why wasn't he feeling good about it?

It had to end and, the longer it carried on, the higher the chances of her getting hurt.

She wanted more than he was ever going to be able to give her.

He wanted a stiff drink. He wanted to punch something. That lack of control was as powerful as a depth charge and he detested the weakness it represented.

'You need to. We had fun but it's time for us to go our separate ways. What will you tell your family? What are your plans moving forward?'

Rosie shrugged and met his dark, shuttered eyes without flinching. Fear of the future gripped her like a vice.

'I'll think of something. It's not your concern and, don't worry, I wouldn't dump you in it. Now, if you don't mind, I think I'll head up.'

'Take care, Rosie. I'll be gone by the time you wake up tomorrow morning.'

CHAPTER TEN

FOR THE FIRST time in her life, the frenzied excitement of a fast-approaching Christmas day left Rosie feeling flat and miserable.

True to his word, Matteo was gone by the time she awoke the following morning. She'd barely slept but she must have dozed off at some point because surely she would have heard him leaving the house? Naturally, he hadn't slept with her, and the bed had felt as vast as an icy ocean. How had she managed to become so accustomed to the warmth of his body next to her in such a short space of time? Didn't she have *any* inbuilt defence mechanisms that could have come to the rescue? How had she been so ill-equipped to deal with this situation?

She stayed at the ski lodge just long enough to pack her things. Her parents had a house-keeper who came to clean when the place was not in use, and usually Rosie would have made sure to do some rudimentary tidying before she arrived, but this time she hadn't the heart to do anything but plaster a phoney smile on her face and do the rounds with all her friends at the hotel and on the ski slopes.

Then she headed back to London, to her parents' apartment, which she had always used as a base whenever she was in the country.

She looked around her through new, wide open eyes. She was a woman in her twenties who had always thought that travelling the world was a courageous and daring way of life. Her sisters, in her view, had been solid, grounded, unadventurous souls who had buried themselves in having careers when there was so much world out there waiting to be explored.

Thanks to Matteo, all those notions had been turned on their head.

Since when had it ever been courageous to live at home with Mum and Dad when you didn't have to? Since when was it a daring decision to live off a trust fund and sneer at the tedium of responsibility?

It was an ordeal to face her entire family when she returned.

She spent two days in London, catching up with friends, seeing everything in a whole new light. Then she headed up to the Cotswolds, where her mother was in the thick of Christmas preparations, bulk-making mince pies and Christmas treats for the entire family while her dad sheepishly read the newspapers and watched from the side-lines.

Emily, Candice and entourage were all going to be spending Christmas Eve at the Cotswold mansion where her parents lived.

'Darling, it's such a shame that that gorgeous young man of yours can't join us for at least some of the Christmas celebrations,' her mother sighed when on the first night they all sat down for a family dinner at the kitchen table. 'Surely he could have spared a day or so even if he had to disappear for Christmas day?'

'Work commitments,' Rosie had muttered vaguely. 'You know how it goes...'

She needed some breathing space before she told her parents that the whirlwind romance had crashed and burned. She planned to tell them the truth. She would reassure them that she didn't need protecting, that she wasn't a kid any more. She had decided that she would return to university to study sports science. The ski season and teaching at the resort had pointed her in the direction which she now intended to go. Lots of mature decisions had been made and that chapter she had talked about had been opened. She just wished she felt better about it because right now, right here, staring at her reflection in the mirror a mere couple of hours before her sisters descended in a flurry of excitement, presents and stockings that would sneakily be hung for the kids once they were asleep, the world felt like a very lonely place.

Downstairs, her mother would be getting everything ready for the meal of the year, the crowning glory that was the turkey for Christmas Day. It would be put in brine and, at the crack of dawn in the morning, it would be all systems go and Rosie would be expected to be her usual self—excitable, up early before everyone else, fussing over the Christmas tree, the food and everything that would need doing before her sisters, the kids and the other halves woke up and trooped downstairs.

Bubbly, sparkling Aunty Rosie was her designated role and she would have to live up to it or else invite curiosity and anxious questioning. All that was going to happen soon enough, post-Christmas Day and Boxing Day, once she had had time to get over some of the raw pain. Once she had got her thoughts in order. Once she could manage to go for five minutes without thinking about him, which she did constantly.

As soon as she started thinking about him, her body did what it was accustomed to doing—it tensed up, all her muscles contracting and her nerves going into overdrive. And her brain did what it had also grown accustomed to doing—it began wandering down all sorts of pointless dead ends marked *what if?* and *if only.*

She was bracing herself for an evening of pretending to be jolly when there was a bang on her bedroom door and her mother pushed it open, giving Rosie just enough time to get her face in happy mode.

'Darling, there's a surprise downstairs for you.' Her mother smiled. She was wearing a red-and-white apron which was dusted with flour. Underneath it, in a pair of jeans and a long-sleeved tee shirt, she looked twenty years younger than she was.

'Father Christmas come early? Drawn by the smell of your mince pies?' Rosie forced a smile and stood up. She was dressed and ready to start the evening in a pair of culottes and a fitted stretchy top with lots of sparkle and glitter, as befitting a Christmas Eve gathering. She was counting on the clothes to give the right impression just in case her expression ended up letting the side down. 'Have the girls and kids arrived already?' She glanced at her watch with a frown. 'It's not yet six. I thought they were going to pile up around seven. Sorry, Mum, I should be downstairs helping you!'

'Don't be silly, Rosie. Too many cooks spoil the broth. And no, your sisters aren't here just yet. No, guess again.'

'I can't guess.'

'Your young man has shown up out of the blue. Isn't that wonderful? He's come bearing gifts, which is sure to go down well with the little ones.'

'What young man?' It took some seconds to register who her mother was talking about but, even when she had, she still couldn't quite believe her ears.

'How many have you got, Rosie?' Her mother chuckled. 'I can't possibly be seen like this. I'm going to have a quick shower—give you two love birds time to catch up. Your father has disappeared down to the pub for a drink so you won't be disturbed!'

Debbie Carter looked at her daughter seriously. 'I'm so thrilled for you, Rosie. You deserve a decent, lovely chap and I think you've struck jackpot with this one. I told him that I thought he was too busy with work to pop up here but he said that work would just have to take a back seat. Not many business moguls adopt that sort of attitude! I despaired of your father back in the day, when he was sometimes far too busy to remember that there was such a thing as *family* waiting for him to appear! Which makes Matteo such a rare find.'

Rosie contorted her face into something she hoped might pass for a smile and not a grimace of despair. Truth to tell, her heart was beating so wildly in her chest that she didn't have time to think about anything much at all.

'Maybe,' she muttered inaudibly. It was too late to climb out of her glittery, sparkly outfit but she felt like a fool as she went downstairs to the sitting room, to where, she had been told, he had been directed with a glass of wine.

And there he was. Behind him, the Christmas tree which she had helped decorate was awash with tiny white lights and heavy with ornaments that went way back to when she and her sisters had all been kids. Rosie could recognise each and every one of them. The curtains of the big bay windows were pulled back and the outside lights illuminated a panorama of stretching gardens and the light fall of snow, nothing like the sweeping fall that had covered the ski slopes, but still somehow graceful and strangely romantic.

Rosie walked over to the window on trembling legs and briskly yanked the curtains shut.

She had to sidestep a ridiculous mound of presents, all professionally wrapped and covering most of the ground by the tree and spreading in front of the sofas.

She had closed the door behind her, because there was never any telling in her parents' house just who could come bombing into any room without warning, and now she turned to him and folded her arms.

'What are you doing here?'

God, he looked so spectacular, so gorgeous, that she could feel her heart going into freefall.

He hadn't shaved and the roughness of dark stubble covered his chin. Looking closer, his eyes were ringed with slight tiredness. She wondered whether all those important deals had been keeping him up at night.

Conscious that she was hardly looking her most sophisticated in her sparkling attire, Rosie remained standing by the window, as tense as a piece of elastic stretched to breaking point. She'd barely had time to get her hair in order when her mother had barged into the bedroom and it fell in feathery, unruly waves around her heart-shaped face.

'I've come…to talk.'

'Talk about what?' She glanced at all the presents strewn on the ground. 'And why have you brought all this stuff?'

'Because it's Christmas.' He smiled crookedly and took a step towards her, but then stopped, as though uncertain.

'You don't do Christmas,' Rosie said scornfully.

'There were a lot of things I never did until I met you,' he said in a low undertone that she had to strain to hear.

'I can't deal with this, Matteo,' Rosie whispered. 'I don't want you here…spoiling Christmas for me. I just can't handle pretending that everything's fine between us in front of my family. We broke up, for good reasons, and I've begun coming to terms with what I'm going to tell everyone—because, as you've seen, they're still in the dark.'

'I…understand.'

'You've ruined everything coming here with all these presents. My family are going to be doubly upset when I break it to them that it's over between us. They're going to be horribly confused because one minute you… you're showing up pretending to be Father

Christmas and, the next minute, you're just a part of my history and you've moved on with your life.'

'Not if I can help it.'

'Don't!'

'Come and sit on the sofa with me. I can't have this conversation standing a hundred miles away from you. I need you...to be closer to me.'

'It's not going to work.'

'I'm not here to try and revive what we had. I haven't come to try and persuade you into carrying on with any charade because I still...want to sleep with you. Because you still haunt my dreams.'

He sat on the sofa and waited, his fabulous eyes focused on her with such unwavering intensity that she could feel her body burning up as she stumbled towards the sofa and sat down, pressed up at one end, because any closer would have made her already fast-dissolving nerves dissolve even faster.

'Rosie.' There was urgent sincerity in his voice and, more than anything else, more even than the brutal impact of his physical presence, that made her still, made her focus her wide blue eyes on his. 'I let you go and I should never have done that.' He raised his hand to halt any interruption, even though she had no intention of interrupting because she had been thoroughly silenced by the tone of his voice. 'I...was afraid.'

'Afraid? *Afraid?* Matteo, there's no way I... I can believe that. Isn't being afraid just one of the hundreds of things you don't *do*?' Bewilderment nudged a way past her defences. She felt as though she was suddenly standing on quicksand.

'Used to be.' He pressed his thumbs briefly over his eyes and then looked at her with none of his usual self-assurance.

Rosie had no intention of melting but she knew that she was straining towards him, closing the gap without really realising it. She had pressed her hands on the squidgy sofa and was leaning forward.

'Don't say anything you don't mean, Matteo.'

'I'm not. This comes from the heart, and if I'm not as fluent as I usually am it's because I'm not accustomed to this sort of speech. Rosie, my life, before I met you, was so well-ordered,' Matteo confessed in a roughened undertone. 'No surprises. Relationships, women... I knew how to deal with both. I never wanted any sort of long-term, committed involvement with anyone and I always made that clear at the start of a relationship. I wasn't raised to see the up sides of forming any emotional attachments.'

Rosie was holding her breath. She reached out to cover his hand with hers, her heart softening even as her head tried to be stern and unforgiving.

He didn't remove his hand. In fact, he curled his fingers into hers and tugged her ever so slightly closer to him so that their knees were touching and she could feel the warmth flowing from his body towards her.

'I wasn't abandoned as a baby,' he said roughly. 'My mother—shockingly, in this day and age—died in childbirth. I know this because I was told when I was old enough by one of the carers at the home. I was raised single-handedly by my father until I was four. I remember him. A kind man—this is simply what I have managed to put together over the years using all the resources at my disposal, including hunting down some of the staff who worked there when I was a child, and people who briefly knew him where he worked. My father died at Christmas. He'd left me with a neighbour so that he could go buy some presents. It was an accident. Poor weather conditions.'

'Matteo!'

'It was a long time ago.' Matteo smiled. 'But

I suppose you could say that the experience toughened me up. I learned very young that no one was going to rescue me. I had to make my own way in the world and I couldn't depend on anyone. I had lost both my parents. My faith in loving anyone had taken a fatal beating.'

'That's why Christmas is the one time of year you avoid,' she said slowly.

'I have pictures. Not many. Memories.' He sighed. 'When I met you, you couldn't have been more different from the women I was accustomed to going for.'

'As you made crystal-clear,' Rosie murmured. Her mind was taken up with images of a young Matteo, lost, confused and bewildered by the abrupt death of his father, abandoned to fate. Her heart constricted and she had to swallow back tears. He did this to her. Showed her sides to him that made him irresistible. Beneath the harsh, controlled front there was so much humanity.

'I got sucked in without really understanding how. A first for me. And then I met your family, all of them, and what I experienced was also a first. I experienced what it felt like to be surrounded by the closeness of people who cared about you. I experienced what it felt like to be a part of something bigger. It was...disorienting.'

'We can overwhelm.'

'In a positive way.' He angled a smile. 'You're very lucky, Rosie, but not as lucky as I am to have met you. What started out as a charade turned into something else very quickly. We became lovers and it was nothing like I'd ever felt before.'

Keep talking, Rosie thought, *please don't stop.*

'It was…unsettling. When you confronted me after meeting Bethany and laid into me because I hadn't defended you, well, it made me take stock of just how far I'd been drawn into a situation that had somehow spiralled out of control. All my old habits kicked back into gear big time.' He grimaced. 'I was programmed not to care, to focus on what was tangible, namely work. You wanted what was not in the brochure and I told myself that it was for the best that things ended, not just for me, but for you as well. I told myself that you deserved better. Maybe, Rosie, you do.'

'Never,' Rosie breathed shakily. 'I met you and you turned my life upside down in five seconds flat. I didn't want to fall in love with you, Matteo, but I just couldn't help myself, even though my head was telling me all the time that I was being an idiot.'

'You fell in love with me.' He flung his

head back for a few seconds, eyes closed, and then when he looked at her there was no doubt in her mind that her feelings for him were returned. The love and tenderness in his eyes brought a lump to her throat. 'I wasn't sure. I'd hoped. Then you left and it felt as though my world had come to an abrupt stop. I was greedy, Rosie. Greedy for you and hungry for the chaos and joy of having an extended family. I thought I'd locked up my heart and thrown away the key, but I was wrong.

'I came here, bearing gifts…lots of them.' He squeezed her slender fingers. 'In a gesture of shameless blackmail. I intended to ingratiate myself until I won you over. Anything, my darling. I realised that I would have done anything.'

He'd brought something else aside from sack-loads of presents but Rosie didn't find that out until later, when the carols were blaring in the background and her entire family was scattered between the living room and the kitchen, with Candice's children weaving between them in a state of high excitement.

He gathered them all in one place and he took out from his pocket that last thing he had brought with him. A little black box.

Rosie watched in stunned silence as he showed her that her beautiful, arrogant, guy…

the guy who claimed to have lost the key to his heart...could be breathtakingly romantic after all.

He knelt in front of her, in front of her entire congregated family—including the kids, who had fallen silent for ten seconds—and he proposed.

And what else could she do but say yes? *Yes, yes, yes!*

EPILOGUE

MATTEO LOOKED DOWN at Rosie from the towering heights of a precariously balanced ladder. In his hand he held a star. In his head he was trying to figure out how he was going to get the damn thing to sit perfectly atop the massive Christmas tree that adorned the living room of the townhouse into which they had moved three months previously.

It wasn't quite the countryside, but neither was it the heart of the city. It was perfectly located in the leafy borough of Richmond.

'Please be careful up there,' Rosie said anxiously. 'You look way too big for that ladder.'

'Finishing touches.' Matteo smiled. 'You want everything to be perfect for when the troops arrive in a week for turkey with all the trimmings, don't you?'

He angled the star, waited until approval from his beloved wife was given, and then slowly dismounted. Then he stood back to look at their creation.

Arm around her, he pulled her gently against him. Outside, the darkness was blocked out by thick curtains. Inside, the glittering lights on the tree and the presents waiting to be handed out to family was a Christmas scene worthy of a postcard. Or a fairy tale. Matteo thought that it was certainly *his* fairy tale.

He'd found his princess, even if he hadn't immediately known it, and he had married her. In record time, a mere few weeks after he had proposed in front of a delighted audience of people who were now as close to him as he could ever have hoped.

He smelled the floral sweetness of Rosie's hair and murmured softly, 'Do you wish we could have returned to the slopes and celebrated our first proper Christmas together there?'

Rosie twisted and looked up at him, smiling.

'You know you put your foot down when I suggested popping over for a few days.' She smiled, reaching up to stroke his face.

'Can you blame me?'

'My darling, I'm six months' pregnant. I think travelling is still allowed.'

Matteo rested his hand on her swollen

stomach and felt it again, that surge of pride, love, tenderness and a fierce need to protect the beautiful woman who had become his wife.

He'd gone from tough, hard-as-nails tycoon to a guy who was happy to admit that he was vulnerable.

'You can't be too careful,' Matteo growled, swivelling her gently so that they were facing one another. He gazed down at her with love. 'But we'll get there. Maybe next year. Maybe next Christmas. Return to the place where all this began.'

'And maybe bump into Bob and Margaret.' Rosie smiled, thinking of the couple who had been almost as thrilled at their wedding as she and Matteo had been themselves. 'I gather from her email that they're getting quite proficient.' She reached up on tiptoe to kiss him and, as always, the touch of his cool lips made her squirm with sudden desire. 'Who knows? You might get there one day.'

'I intend to.' Matteo grinned and deepened his kiss, his hand curving over her breast, caressing it and knowing that she would be wet for him. 'I can't have you teaching our kids how to ski so that they can taunt their old man that they're better than him on the slopes.'

'In that case, we can get cracking as soon as this baby arrives.'

'And until then…' he ushered her over to the sofa and settled her into it as delicately as if she was a piece of priceless china '…feet up, young lady. I can do more than just stick a star on a tree. Your wish is my command.'

'You're here, Matteo.' Rosie looked at him lovingly. 'I have no more wishes.'

* * * * *

If you enjoyed
The Italian's Christmas Proposition
*you're sure to enjoy these other stories
by Cathy Williams!*

The Tycoon's Ultimate Conquest
Contracted for the Spaniard's Heir
Marriage Bargain with His Innocent
Shock Marriage for the Powerful Spaniard

Available now!